# INDULGE ME

## EMILIA ROSE

Editor: Jovana Shirley, Unforeseen Editing, www.unforeseenediting.com

Proofreading: Heart Full of Reads, Kirsten Clower, Tina Franco

Emilia Rose

emiliarosewriting@gmail.com

*To all the girls who wished their best friends' dads were sweet enough to love.*

# PART 1

# CHAPTER 1

MICHAEL

*M*ia.

There were a hundred thoughts rushing through my head as I washed all our sex off my body, but she was the only one I cared about. Hearing those three little words the other night had been one of the best things to happen to me in a long time.

I shut the water off and stepped out of the shower. Mia telling me she loved me had been enough for me to go out after work and start looking for something perfect for her. I wiped some water off my legs, threw the towel over my shoulder, and walked into our bedroom, naked, to open up my dresser.

The black box was buried deep within my clothes, where Mia would never find it. I drew my fingers against the leather and took a deep breath. She was young, and I didn't want to rush my relationship with her. But I had never felt this sure about anything in my entire life.

"Michael," Mia called from somewhere in the house.

I shut the drawer, my heart pounding, thinking about how long I would have to wait until I knew she was ready for something like … *that*. I wanted to at least repair my relationship with Melissa before I asked Mia to—

"I don't think you should come in," Mia said, her voice unsure.

I wiped the last of the water off my chest and raised a brow, tying the towel around my waist and walking into the hall. I swore if Mason was here, trying to stir up trouble, I—

I stopped mid-thought and stared down the stairs at the woman who had ruined my entire life.

Linda stood there with the most menacing smirk I had ever seen, walked right up the stairs toward me, and drew her fingers over my chest. "Michael, you're home."

Immediately, I stepped away from her and glanced down the stairs to make sure Mia was okay. Mia glanced between us, her expression faltering and turning into a mix of hurt, betrayal, and anger. It hurt me to see her so … so sad.

"What the fuck are you doing here?" I asked.

But of course she was here. She had to ruin every good thing in my life. Everything had been going great, better than it ever had. Mia's mother was recovering. Melissa had come over once this week. Mia was finally able to focus on school again … and now, Linda was fucking back to screw with my life.

"I didn't invite you into my house."

"Mia did," she said, stepping closer to me.

Mia crossed her arms over her chest. "No, I didn't."

"Get out," I said again, being careful not to touch her. God knew she'd try to turn this back on me and say I was harassing her or something.

She swung her purse around like a madwoman and laughed. "Oh, Michael, what's wrong? I just wanted to visit my husband while he's in a good mood. Melissa told me that you had a new girlfriend."

My nostrils flared. I should've never fucking married her. Linda was too unstable.

She glanced down at Mia. "Is this her? You're fucking a girl young enough to be your own daughter?"

I gulped, hating how bad it sounded.

"Is it because she has a nice body? Is that the only reason you went after her? She's young and impressionable? Easy to manipulate?"

I flared my nostrils. She was trying to rile me up, and it was fucking working.

Mia shifted uncomfortably under her gaze. Everything Linda had said out loud wasn't true. Sure, it'd started as physical attraction, but that wasn't why I was dating Mia, and it wasn't why I loved her either.

"Get out of my house," I said.

"Our house, Michael," she said. "Don't you remember when we used to live here together? And now, you have a young whore living here in place of me."

She tilted her head, and I could smell the booze on her.

I clenched my hands into fists. *Control yourself, Michael. She's fucking with you.*

She stepped closer to me, and I stepped back.

"Take one more fucking step, Linda, and I'm calling the police."

"Calling the police for what?" she asked, testing me. "Sleeping with an underage girl?"

"I'm twenty-two," Mia said, seizing the railing. "Old enough to make my own decisions."

Linda hummed amusingly. "Sure, *twenty-two...* that's what we'll call you."

"If you come close to me or Mia again, I will get a restraining order against you." And I meant it. I could deal with her craziness, but I wasn't going to put Mia's life in danger. "Leave."

Linda narrowed her eyes at me, and then she walked down

the stairs, out the damn door, and to her car. I shut the door behind her and growled under my breath. She was a fucking bitch who'd do anything to ruin my life like she had ruined hers. She had to try to bring me down with her.

"Michael," Mia whispered as soon as the door closed. Something about her was off, as she wouldn't look me in the eye. "Michael, you know I love you. I don't want to get in the way of … *anything*."

"Don't think you're the problem, Mia, because you're not."

"I don't want her to hurt you. You're respected in the city. If people find out that we're dating, they're going to look at you differently. And …" A look of fear crossed her face. "What if she says something about us that isn't true? What if she says that we've been together since I was in high school?"

I gulped. Linda would spread those rumors around town. But I didn't want Mia to worry about this. Linda was my problem, and I would deal with her.

"It doesn't matter what everyone else thinks," I said, pulling her closer to me. There was hesitation in her stature, but she eventually relaxed in my arms and wrapped her arms around me. "The truth matters, Mia, and you and I know that best."

# CHAPTER 2

MIA

*A*fter Melissa's mother had left yesterday morning, I had felt off. Something about the way she'd barged into the house made me feel much lesser than her. She had been the woman before me, had almost spent more time with Michael than I had been alive, knew more about him than I did.

"Hello?!" Serena said, waving a hand in front of my face. "You going to finish your work, so we can hang out, or no?"

I glanced down at the computer with my psychology work on it and frowned. The sunlight flooded in through her apartment window, and I could hear Victor and Damien playing video games in the other room.

"Sorry, I was thinking."

"Daydreaming about Michael?" she asked, brow raised.

"Just about everything." I typed some words into my document and submitted it through the online system to my professor.

I had been taking summer classes, and I wished it were over

already. Melissa and Serena had both graduated last semester, and I had been so caught up with Mom's health and everything else that I had to drop two classes.

So, here I was, in the middle of summer, studying and writing stupid reports.

"I'm so happy you're graduating soon!" Serena said, squealing. She wrapped her arms around my shoulders and smiled down at my computer. "It might not be on time, but so close!"

I sighed down at all my work I had to do. "Yeah, I wish I'd had some time for myself, some time to actually enjoy college, but I wouldn't change anything."

"Well, let's take a break." She pulled me to the bed. "Have you heard from Melissa?"

I arched a brow and glanced over at her. "She came over to see Michael once a few days ago when I was visiting Mom. He hasn't said much about her since. I think they're talking, but not as much as they used to talk."

She grabbed her phone and scrolled through her Contacts to Melissa's name. There were some unanswered texts from her, some answered ones. I frowned at the phone and at how desperate Melissa seemed over text to talk to someone. Part of me felt so bad about it.

"Are you going to text her back?"

Serena shrugged and sighed again. "I don't know. I don't want to after what she did."

"She won't talk to me. Maybe you can get it through her head that Mason isn't good for her. I don't want her to be abused too." I wiggled my toes and gulped. "I think that might be good. You can tell me if she seems different."

I knew Melissa wouldn't say anything about being used by him. She was a headstrong girl and didn't take anyone's shit … but she seemed different with Mason. Like he had a magical dick for her or something.

"Are you sure?" Serena asked. "I'll go get coffee with her. But I don't know if I'll ever be able to be friends with her again. How could I trust her with Damien if she did that to you?"

I sighed and rested my head against her shoulder. She had a point. At least Melissa wouldn't try to come on to my man now. I smirked and wrinkled my nose. Okay, not my best joke, but still funny.

"Mason has been texting me," I said.

She sat up and widened her eyes. "Are you being serious? What a sicko."

"If you go out with her, tell her. I have screenshots."

She giggled and lay back down. "Of course you do."

After a few moments of silence, I said, "They moved my mom from the hospital to St. Barbars yesterday."

My stomach felt light with butterflies. I hadn't had a chance to go see her, but I was so happy that she was getting better. It was a slow process, but it was happening. Her memory was still shot. She didn't remember that I had visited her the day before, and it made me sad, but James kept up a happy attitude, which was more than helpful.

"Yay!" Serena said. "That's amazing news!"

I smiled. "I think she's going to do better there. She has someone else in her life now who will keep her strong. And she's not living in that disgusting assisted living place anymore."

"You think she's getting it on with James?" Serena asked, giggling.

I playfully slapped her on her shoulder and stared up at the ceiling. "Ew."

"What? She'd better be getting it. That woman has been through hell."

My nose scrunched up, yet I let out a soft laugh. James seemed like a great guy and had been visiting her quite often. I wouldn't doubt that they'd done something together, but in the hospital? I shivered. Goodness, I hoped not. I lay in the same bed as her some days.

My phone buzzed, and I lifted it to see Michael's name.

**Michael: Want to visit your mother at St. Barbars when I get off work?**

I glanced over at Serena, who was smiling from ear to ear.

"Hey, go get your man. You don't stay in this honeymoon phase forever."

Victor and Damien started yelling from the living room about a video game that they couldn't seem to win.

She glanced over at the door and let out a laugh. "I have my hands full here, anyway."

# CHAPTER 3

MIA

"*W*hy'd you take the bus and not my car?" Michael asked, brow raised at me.

I slid into the passenger side of his car and raised my brow back at him, giving him that *you know why* expression.

He tilted his head at me and pulled me into a kiss. "You're not a bad person for taking the car whenever you need it. I don't care as long as you don't steal the thing, Mia."

Serena waved us off from the sidewalk, wiggling her brows at me as I looked at her in the rearview mirror.

I tossed my backpack into the backseat and turned on the music, relaxing. "Your father is there too, isn't he?"

Michael merged onto the highway and drove for a bit. "He is. Do you want to meet him?"

My stomach tightened, and I fumbled with my fingers. I hadn't ever met someone's parents before. Did he know how old I was? Michael had told me not to mind that, but ... it still felt a bit weird for me.

"Sure," I said.

He turned off the highway and drove into the St. Barbars' parking lot. It was a huge building with colorful, blooming tulips lining the white cement sidewalks. I smiled at it, knowing that this place was definitely better than the last place Mom had lived in.

Michael took my hand and guided me into the building. Even the inside seemed so lively. There wasn't that feel of death and despair I'd felt every time I walked into Orangegate Assisted Living. There was hope on everyone's face, even the patients'.

When we walked into the building, the nurse at the front desk smiled at Michael.

"Michael, how are you?" she asked. Her eyes flickered to me, and she grinned. "You must be his daughter."

I glanced up at Michael, lost for words. Michael parted his lips and pressed them back together, glancing down at me and squeezing my hand tighter.

"This is Mia," he said, quickly recovering. "She's my girlfriend."

The nurse blushed, her expression dropping. She formed an O with her lips and quickly shuffled through some paperwork to get us signed in. But even when we signed in and started our walk to Mom's room, I could feel her staring at us.

When we were out of sight, Michael leaned down closer to me. "Damn, do I look that old?" he asked, trying to lighten the mood.

I smiled up at him and knocked twice on the mahogany door to Mom's room.

"Come in!" she called, sounding livelier than she had a few days ago.

When we entered, she plastered a huge smile on her face.

"Sweetheart! How are you doing?" she asked, stroking her fingers against my hair.

I placed my hand on her knee and sat down next to her on

the bed.

"Great," I said. "Started school a few weeks ago. I have two more classes to finish."

Michael placed a hand on my shoulder, nodded to her wheelchair, and smiled at her. "You want to go out? There's a garden in the back that I think you'll lo—"

"Hey! What's going on here? Having a party without me?" James walked into the room with a bunch of roses in his hand. He squeezed Michael's shoulder and placed the roses on the side table. "Eden, feeling better?"

Mom's eyes widened. "I haven't seen you in years."

"I saw you yesterday, darling."

I rested my head on Michael's shoulder. "What about that walk?"

Mom nodded, and James bent over to try to help her into her wheelchair, but Michael stepped in, so he wouldn't throw out his back. I pushed Mom through the garden behind St. Barbars and let her sit out in the sun for a bit. She'd always loved to suntan when I was younger. She could do it for hours upon hours, getting a tan or burning like a lobster. It was either one or the other.

She waved off James and Michael, telling them we needed some girl time, like she had done for the past few weeks.

"So, you and Michael." She raised her brows at me and smiled widely. "What's going on between you two? Are you and he official? Does everyone know? How did Melissa take it?"

I frowned at her. It was always the same questions every day, and I hoped that she'd get better soon, but I wasn't complaining. I'd take this over never seeing her. It was just sad.

"She's taking it rough," I said like I always did, not really wanting to get into it. Just the thought of Melissa made me both angry and unbelievably heartbroken. "I hope she comes around and starts to talk to Michael again, but I'm not sure it'll be anytime soon."

EMILIA ROSE

"She'll come around," she said, clasping my hand. "They always do." She paused for a long moment, checked behind her to make sure the guys weren't near, and then asked me the one question I'd never thought I'd hear come out of her mouth. "Are you taking birth control?"

My cheeks warmed. "Yes. Why?"

She eyed me for a few moments, her gaze drifting down my body so slowly, as if she was analyzing me or something. After a couple moments, she shrugged. "No reason. Just wondering."

I arched an eyebrow and decided to drop the subject as Michael and James approached us, talking about the new buildings being constructed in the city. I smiled at him and wheeled Mom back to her room. James followed us, talking Mom's ear off about how he couldn't wait to take her on that vacation, how they'd finally get some relaxation after all this stress, which made her smile that big smile she used to have before Dad started drinking.

"Well, we're off. We have to go visit Michael's father," I said to Mom.

She pulled me into a big hug. "See you soon, sweetheart."

Michael grabbed my hand and led me to the opposite side of the building, where his father's room was. When we walked into the room, his father was lying in his bed and watching some angsty soap opera that Dad used to watch when I was young. I remembered sitting in his lap with a big bowl of Fruity Pebbles, watching women throw water in each other's face and men who had so much of their own damn drama.

When he saw us, he smiled at Michael, then at me. "Michael, you brought someone for me." He wiggled his eyebrows at him, and I stifled a laugh. "What's your name?"

"Mia."

He gave Michael the eye and tried sitting up in his bed, his arms too weak to support himself. Before he could collapse back on the bed, Michael pulled him into a seated position, and I smiled at him. If he was this patient with older adults, I wondered how good he would be with ki—

*No. Not right now, Mia.*

After about fifteen minutes, his father got tired of talking. We left him with his soap opera and turned the light off.

"Your father's nice," I said, shutting the door behind us.

He took a steadying breath and pushed his hands in his pockets, as if he didn't agree. "He is now. Hasn't always been." Michael turned his lips up. "Threw me out of the house when Melissa was born. One of those strict, *doesn't take any shit* fathers."

I intertwined our fingers. Despite everything he had been through, Michael had turned out to be so successful. Being thrown out of his house, taking care of a baby when he was young, dealing with all of his ex-wife's shit … it made me think that I could be that successful one day too.

"I tried to be different when raising Melissa," Michael said. "I wanted her to learn responsibility, but now, she barely talks to me."

I frowned at him, feeling the brunt of his guilt. It was because of me that he felt shitty. I didn't know if Michael would've ever thrown Melissa out if she had cheated on her boyfriend with someone else.

"I'm sorry," I said, rubbing his bicep. "She'll come around. Maybe not soon, but she will."

As we walked into the lobby, the woman at the counter looked over at us again. There were other nurses this time, staring at me like they were disgusted, their noses wrinkling, eyes narrowing. I glanced over at them and curled my fingers tighter around Michael's bicep, not wanting to stir up trouble here for visiting.

I hated to think this, but I knew it was only bound to get worse than this. People would continue to stare. They'd continue to judge. And with Michael's ex-wife, they'd start to hear the rumors about us.

# CHAPTER 4

MIA

*W*hen we left St. Barbars, the sky was a midnight blue already. I slid into the passenger side of Michael's car and let him drive aimlessly through the city. He rested his hand on my thigh and took an exit we hadn't ever been down, but I didn't complain. I loved going on adventures with him even if it was to the grocery store at eleven p.m. It didn't matter to me.

"I have a dinner party with some people from the office on Friday night." He turned onto a dirt street and drove into the wooded area. He paused for a moment and glanced over at me. "Do you want to come with me?"

I gulped. Michael worked as a principal architect on the Vestige Towers Project in the center of the city, which was projected to become the next hub in the nation within the next few years. I hadn't met anyone from his work before, and to say I was nervous was an understatement.

He glanced over at me and chuckled deeply. "It'll be fine, Mia. It's just dinner."

But I couldn't stop imagining about what his coworkers would think of us. Those ladies at the assisted living center surely had their opinions on our relationship. Hell, the receptionist had thought I was his daughter, for Christ's sake. What would his coworkers think?

I grasped his hand and squeezed it tightly. "Do they know about me?"

"Of course they do."

"No, I mean … do they know about my age?" I asked, sucking on my cheek.

It was one thing to tell his coworkers he had a new girlfriend. It was another for him to show up at a fancy dinner party with someone half his age.

He sighed through his mouth. "How many times do I have to tell you that I don't care what anyone else thinks of this age gap between us? I'm not going to let them make my choices for me. It's me and you, Mia."

There was a small clearing ahead. He drove into it and parked his car. My eyes widened at the entire view of the city—the sparkling lights from the Vestige Towers, the hum from Market Square, even some city workers exiting their buildings this late at night.

I glanced back over at him and smiled. "Me and you," I whispered.

Michael thrust a hand into his left pocket and fumbled around for a few moments, staring out the windshield at the entire city glimmering against the dark night sky.

Between our seats, my phone buzzed, and Mason's name flashed on the screen.

**Mason: Let's meet up.**

I froze on the spot. Michael tensed next to me, his hand on my thigh tightening.

"Meet up?" he asked me, trying to keep his voice steady, but I could hear the hurt in it.

I parted my lips. *God, what is with us and crazy exes?*

"Why does Mason want to meet up with you?" Michael asked, pulling away from me.

When his hand left my skin, I felt like I had betrayed him. I should've told him about Mason sooner, but with the drama with Melissa's mother, I had forgotten. Or maybe I hadn't had it in me to add another problem to our relationship.

"Have you been texting him?" he asked.

"No," I said strongly. "He has been texting me, and I have been ignoring him."

"Why haven't you deleted his number?" Hurt crossed his face. "Or blocked him?"

"For Melissa."

As soon as the words left my mouth, it sounded like such a shitty excuse. But it was the truth. I glanced at the stars, then back at him.

"I want you and Melissa to speak again. I want you to have a good relationship because my dad and I have a shitty one. She needs someone who will support her emotionally." I held his hand and trailed my finger across his knuckles. "I don't care if she never talks to me again. We have our own problems. But I still want her to be safe, and if this"—I held up my phone and scrolled to the hundreds of unanswered messages from Mason— "will prove it to her, then I'm going to use it."

I didn't want him to worry or to think I was cheating, but I had to be honest with Michael. This wasn't about me. I didn't give a fuck about Mason texting me, didn't need to keep his messages or pictures to reminisce on old times. I needed them to try to protect Melissa whenever she wanted to talk to me again.

Michael took his hand out of his pocket and rested it on the steering wheel. "Okay," he said cautiously.

I frowned at him and cupped his face in my hand, trying to figure out how to prove to him that Mason meant nothing to me.

"If you want me to block him, I will," I said.

But I knew deep down that blocking his number wouldn't stop Mason from bothering me. He'd take it out on someone else like Melissa, or he'd show up at Michael's front door to try to get me to talk to him again.

Michael stayed quiet for a while and clutched my hand tightly in his. "Promise me you love me more than him," he whispered.

"I love you, Michael, more than I have ever loved any other man." I pushed a strand of hair off his forehead.

It hurt me to see him hurt. It was usually men who hurt me. Being on the other side of the pain sucked almost as much for me because I knew what it felt like.

"I would do anything to keep us together." I pressed my lips on his and crawled into his lap, resting my knees on either side of his legs. *"Anything."*

# CHAPTER 5

MIA

"*Y*ou are mine." He seized my hips and held me down against him, letting me feel his bulge through his pants.

He drove his hips up, and I rested my hands on his shoulders and squeezed, my pussy tightening at how big he felt.

"All mine."

"Yours," I breathed, bucking my hips back and forth to ride him through his pants. My panties were soaked, my cunt warm.

At that moment, there wasn't a doubt in my mind about us. I wanted to spend the rest of my life with him and not care about what anyone else thought.

He slipped a hand between my legs and into my skirt to rub my clit. "Every part of you is mine, Mia." He grasped my jaw gently in his hand and pushed it to the side, pressing his lips below my ear and leaving a trail of hot kisses down the side of my neck.

I slid a hand between us and stroked him through his pants,

feeling his cock, imagining him pounding it inside of me. When he pulled down the strap of my tank top, exposing my breast, he placed his mouth on it, and I threw my head back and moaned.

"Every part of me," I repeated.

He bit down on my nipple, sending a wave of ecstasy through my body. I sunk my hand into his hair, arching my back and trying to breathe steadily. His tongue swirled around my nipple again, and then he tugged on it, becoming rougher with me.

When I couldn't hold myself back anymore, I undid his button and zipper and pulled out his stiffness. I spit on my hand and stroked him with it, needing him inside of me.

"Feel how hard it is for you?" he asked into my ear, rubbing his fingers faster. "Only you can make me feel this good." He slipped a finger into my pussy, the heel of his hand hitting my clit. "Only *you* can make me this hard."

God, I was going to …

My pussy tightened around his fingers.

Going to …

I moaned loudly when he bent his fingers against my G-spot.

He groaned and readjusted himself, hooking a finger under my panties and moving them to the side. "Slide yourself down onto my cock and tell me how good it feels inside of you."

My legs were still tingling, the pleasure washing through me, but I positioned myself above him and let him slide into me until my hips were against his. He ground his hips up into mine even more.

After snaking his hand around the front of my throat, he pulled me closer to him. "Tell me."

"You make me feel …" I gulped as he started to pound up into me, making me unable to even concentrate. "Feel so …"

"Feel so what, Mia?" he asked, pulling down my other tank top strap and letting my other breast fall out of it.

Every time he pumped into me, my breasts would bounce against his chest, my nipples becoming more and more taut.

"You make me feel so good."

He stared up at me like I was the only thing that mattered, his lips parted and eyes hazy. Overcome with lust … or maybe that was love. "Do you want to come again?"

"Please," I said, my voice coming out so desperate.

He sucked one of my nipples back into his mouth and tugged on it, ramming fast and deep into my pussy. "Tell me you're mine again," he said against my breast. "I want to hear it."

I threw my head back, moving my hips with his. "I'm you—"

"Look at me when you say it."

I stared down at him, my pussy clenching hard, and grabbed his shoulders. "I'm yours, Michael."

He groped my tits and thrust up. The pressure rose higher and higher in my core, and I curled my toes, feeling a world of emotion wash over me. After a few moments, he wrapped his arms around my body, buried his face into the crook of my neck, and stilled inside of me, his thick cum pumping into me.

He stayed quiet for a few moments, then said, "I want to spend my life with you."

# CHAPTER 6

MIA

Michael wanted to spend his life with me.

As soon as the words had left his mouth, everything inside me had felt so light.

I stared up at my psychology professor, unable to focus on anything but the other night. It had been one of the best feelings in the world.

My phone buzzed in my pocket, pulling me out of my thoughts. I cleared my throat and sat up taller in my seat, focusing on the slides Dr. Xiao had on the screen about dissociative identity disorder.

On my computer, I typed every word she said, knowing that it'd all be on the exam. After another fifteen minutes and two more phone messages later, she finally released the class. I hurriedly packed all my belongings, wanting to get a head start on my homework.

"Mia," Dr. Xiao called before I could sneak out of the room.

I shoved the last of my work into my backpack and walked over to her desk.

"How are you doing? Your mother?"

"She's doing good," I said, nodding.

Dr. Xiao was the professor of one of the classes I'd had to drop last semester because of Mom's sudden hospitalization. She was one of the most caring professors on this campus I'd met.

Dr. Xiao leaned against her desk, arms crossed, giving me that look. "And you?"

I gave her a small smile. "I'm doing better. I …"

There was so much I wanted to say but didn't have the confidence to. She wouldn't judge me at all for anything, but I didn't know if it was appropriate to bring up my drama.

"It's okay to not be okay. I can tell your mind has been wandering all morning."

I glanced down at my shoes. "I have a lot I'm dealing with."

"Care to share? I have some time before my next class."

"Just my ex-boyfriend, my mom, my best friend …" *My current boyfriend's ex-wife, who also happens to be my best friend's mom.* "College drama. That's all it is."

She raised a brow, giving me a *I don't believe you one bit* look, and rubbed my shoulder. "If you ever need to talk, I'm here for you."

After nodding once more to say good-bye, I walked out of the room and pulled out my phone. I didn't think that Dr. Xiao would understand the type of drama I had gotten myself into. It was more than some petty college drama. I fucked and had fallen in love with my best friend's dad and was facing the consequences.

*Three unread messages from Mom.*

**Mom: Good morning, sweetheart. I hope you're working hard in class today. You make me so proud.**

**Mom: Why don't you come by today? ;)**

**Mom: Sorry, last message was for James!!!**

I scrunched up my nose and stifled a laugh. Mom was definitely getting it on with James in the assisted living center. I had no doubts about it after *that* text. I typed her a quick message about going to Michael's work party this weekend and walked toward the Dunkin' Donuts downtown.

It was by far my favorite place to do homework. It was relatively quiet during the day, and the doughnuts smelled so damn good. My phone buzzed again.

**Mom: Going to a work party? Things must be getting pretty serious. ;)**

**Me: I'm just … nervous.**

**Mom: About what? Seems like Michael really wants you to meet his coworkers.**

I stared at the phone, not knowing how to reply, and frowned.

**Me: Worried about what they'll think about me.**

**Mom: People are going to judge you, no matter what. Don't let it get in the way of your happiness.**

I pushed my phone back into my pocket. I knew not to let people get in the way, but it was still difficult. Something deep down told me that they'd judge me. It wouldn't be to my face, but behind my back. So many men were pigs, and they would think I was just some toy to Michael, like Linda had basically suggested.

But I couldn't let that stand in my way. Michael had said he wanted to spend his life with me, and I wanted nothing more than to spend my life with him. I would try not to let the rumors get in the way, but … it was difficult after being screwed up by Mason.

It would take some time to love truly—without pain, without insecurity, without all these thoughts rushing through my head. I didn't want to push them too much on Michael. I needed to deal with them myself.

I slipped into a Dunkin' Donuts, ordered a lemonade, and grabbed an orange from the bunch of fruit by the registers, deciding on something healthier than another Boston cream doughnut. It was more crowded than usual, but I needed to get some schoolwork done, so I broke out my computer and started on all the homework I had due tomorrow.

Psych. Psych. And more psych.

It was easy stuff, just so much filler work that it was driving me crazy.

My mind wandered to Dr. Xiao and how I should've told her about everything. She lived a couple streets down from Michael. I had seen her walking her dog with her husband, who looked much older than she was, around our neighborhood the other day. If she didn't know we were together already, she would probably find out soon.

Maybe it would be nice to have someone take a fresh look at all the drama. A different perspective that wouldn't make me feel so … so … inclined to shake off these rumors. Because, damn, was it tiring.

After another half hour, I pulled out my phone and tapped on Michael's name in my messages. I knew he was busy at work, but I wanted to forget about everything for a bit. So, I scrolled through my photos until I found the perfect one that I knew would set him off and clicked Send.

# CHAPTER 7

MICHAEL

*J*im, one of my coworkers, clicked on another slide in his presentation about the interior of the towers we were designing. Though I should've been fully engrossed in the PowerPoint slides, I couldn't stop thinking about Mia.

The way she'd lit up when I told her I wanted to spend my life with her... God, it made me feel so fucking good inside. I hadn't felt like that ever. It only made my decision to ask her that complicated question all the more clear.

Hell, I was going to do it last night. But after seeing Mason's text to her, I hadn't had it in me. I'd thought that maybe this wasn't what she wanted. I wanted to give us some more time, and I knew I needed to wait until Melissa and I were back on good terms.

My phone buzzed on the table, and Mia's name with an image popped up. I pulled the phone off the table and onto my lap. The phone buzzed again with the message: **I need your help.** I stared down at it for a few moments, debating on whether I wanted to open the message during a meeting, and then against my better judgment, I opened it up.

Dressed in a lacy black set of lingerie, Mia lay in our bed, biting her lip gently, her fingers touching the front of her panties. Almost immediately, I felt myself get hard, my cock aching to be inside of her. I clenched my jaw and shifted uncomfortably in my seat.

She was sexy, so fucking sexy.

I sucked in a deep breath and put the phone into my pocket, focusing on the blank notebook in front of me. My dick felt like it was pulsing, and all I could imagine was Mia sliding herself on it. Her walls clamping down tightly around me, pussy wrapped around me like she wanted nothing more.

My dick became stiffer, and I pulled my seat closer to the table and told myself to relax. But it was no use. I couldn't think of anything but her. Maybe I should excuse myself, go to the restroom, and jerk off to her picture.

Jim cleared his throat and turned back to the group. I tried my best to keep my attention on him, thinking about anything to get rid of my boner, of these thoughts of tasting every inch of her. Of putting her right on my desk and fucking her senseless. Of pushing her against one of these floor-to-ceiling windows and pounding into her from behind, her tits flush against the glass, her eyes wide with excitement.

The meeting dragged on for another fifteen minutes, yet I couldn't get her off my mind. As soon as Jim finished his presentation, I grabbed my notebook and laptop, resting them in front of my crotch so nobody could see the bulge in my gray suit pants, and hurried out of the room.

After setting my things down at my desk, I took my wallet and phone, dialing Mia's number.

She answered on the first ring, a tinge of playfulness in her voice. "Hello? Who's this?"

"Where are you?" I asked over the phone, desperate to have her.

God, she knew exactly how to get to me, how to make me want her so badly that I'd considered excusing myself from one of the most important meetings of the year.

"Did you like my picture?" she asked. I could hear the smile in her voice.

I glanced around the office and walked toward the windows, where it was quieter. "Fuck, I loved it." The city below was packed with people rushing down the sidewalks to grab a quick lunch. "I'm hard just thinking about you, Mia."

"Dirty talk at work, Michael?" she teased.

I chuckled. "Where are you?"

"Downtown, studying."

"Meet me at Lucian's in five minutes. I need you." And then I hung up the phone and hurried to the elevators for my lunch break.

It took me exactly four minutes to get to Lucian's—a chic restaurant with an outdoor bar, right in the city center.

She was waiting at the entrance, her thin blue dress fitting perfectly to her body. Most of the outdoor tables were taken already, so the hostess brought us toward a table inside the restaurant, which was significantly less busy.

We ordered our food, and I tried to keep my hands off of her until the waitress left because once I touched her, I wouldn't be able to stop. The waitress gave us our drinks, and Mia scooted closer to me in the booth, bare leg grazing against mine.

I slid my hand up her leg and slipped it under her dress, fingers finding her underwear. She spread her legs apart under the table, giving me better access and letting me rub them against her wet panties.

"I've been waiting for this all day," she said.

I drew my fingernail across her underwear, right down her fold, then flicked it against her clit. Her body jerked in the seat, and she grasped the table, pulling herself in and whimpering.

"Say my name." I hooked a finger inside her underwear and pulled it to the side.

She took an unsteady breath through her mouth, nails digging into my thigh. "Michael," she cried, uneasily looking around the restaurant to make sure nobody was watching us.

She leaned back, and I pulled her thigh over mine, making her spread her legs even more for me.

"You like that, don't you?" My gaze fell to her tits, her taut nipples pressing through the dress. The dress was so thin that I could almost see everything, and it made me even harder. "Not wearing a bra for me today?"

She pursed her lips together, gazing down at her nipples and then back at me. "I wasn't going to wear any panties either, but thought you might want to take them back to work with you today."

God, she didn't even have to try.

"Don't test me, Mia," I said tensely, slipping a finger into her pussy and feeling it tighten around me. It was pulsing over and over, and all I wanted was to be inside of her. I slipped another finger inside her, feeling her get tighter. "Because I will bend you right over this table and take you."

She whimpered, sucking her lower lip between her teeth. "I want you to make me come here," she said. "I want to hold back my screams, to feel my pussy pulsing around you."

I gulped, feeling her get even wetter. I seized her hand and placed it on the bulge in my pants. Without hesitation, she undid my belt and zipper and pulled out my cock in the middle of the damn restaurant.

"God, I wish I could suck you off right now." She stroked me, not knowing what she was doing to me. "Wish I could take all of you deep down my throat, wish you'd make me a gagging, teary-eyed mess."

"Fuck," I whispered, thrusting my fingers into her. "Tug on your nipples for me."

She widened her eyes, surprise evident on her face, and then like a good girl, she took one of her nipples between her fingers and tugged harshly as I made a come-hither motion inside of her.

Her lips parted, and she stared down at her lap, holding back her moans. "God ... Mich—" Her legs trembled wildly around me, and she tried to push them together, but I didn't stop. "Oh my gosh, Michael."

Her hand moved just as quickly up and down my length, and I knew I was so fucking close to the edge. But I couldn't come, not here. I'd ruin my clothes and have to go back to work in them.

After a few moments, when she finally settled down enough to stop shaking, I pulled my fingers out of her and gripped her wrist. "Mia, stop. We can't do this right now," I said.

But she didn't stop stroking me. Instead, she stroked me faster and faster.

"Imagine my pussy this tight around you," she whispered to me.

"We can't ..." My dick pulsed. "Can't—"

"My pussy lips wrapped right around you, taking all your cum inside me." She placed a kiss on my jaw. "I know you love to fill me up, to claim what's yours, to watch your cum drip down my thighs."

I gripped her wrist. "Mia, stop."

Yet I didn't pull her away from me because it felt too fucking good. Instead, I grabbed a napkin from the table because Mia wasn't going to stop.

"Mia, I'm going to—"

She glanced around once more, and then dipped her head, taking me all in her mouth. As soon as my dick hit the back of her warm, tight throat, I came inside of her, bucking my hips and trying not to groan.

She bobbed her head back and forth for a moment, then pulled off of me, wiping some cum off the corner of her lip and sticking it into her mouth. She sat back in her seat and smirked at me, and I knew I had a fucking keeper.

# CHAPTER 8

MIA

*a*fter kissing Michael good-bye, I pulled my backpack onto my shoulders and walked down the sidewalk toward Serena's house, where I'd parked my car this morning. I felt like I was walking on top of the world after sucking Michael off in the middle of a restaurant, taking his cum in my mouth so it wouldn't tarnish his pants.

Just when I felt like nothing could ruin my mood after that bomb *public* orgasm, I stopped dead in my tracks when I saw Mason leaning against Michael's car.

I gulped, knowing that nobody was home at Serena's place. Serena was at her internship, and Damien had gotten a job as a junior engineer downtown. Neither would be back until five tonight. I grasped my cell phone tightly. If something went down, I would be calling the freaking police.

"What are you doing here?" I asked, slowly approaching the opposite side of the car.

He gave me his best forced smile. "I wanted to talk, and you wouldn't pick up your phone."

"Maybe that's because I don't want to talk to you."

He let out a loud sigh and took a step around the car toward me. I moved back, wanting to keep as much space between us as I could. I didn't know what the fuck he was up to, but I wasn't about to put myself in danger.

"Mia, don't do that. I just want to talk." He took another step, and so did I. "I'm not going to do anything to you. I swear."

I crossed my arms over my chest and squeezed my phone tighter in my hand. "Well, you can talk from all the way over there. No need to get any closer to me unless you want me to call the police."

He snorted but didn't move any closer. "What are you going to call the police for? Me still loving you?"

I laughed. "Loving me? You never loved me. If you loved me even in the slightest, you wouldn't have flirted with any girl who had a nice pair of tits, you wouldn't have slept with my best friend for months, and you wouldn't have made me think you loved me by caring about my mom."

The expression on his face didn't change, but it did falter for a single moment. "Come on, Mia. Are you seriously still hung up over that when you had a thing for Melissa's dad the entire time we were dating?"

"I didn't have a thing for her dad for the entirety of our relationship."

He raised his brows. "So, you didn't find him attractive? You didn't fantasize about him?"

I stayed quiet. Truth was … I had had a thing for him for *longer* than Mason and I were together. Serena and I would gush about him in high school, would dream about getting with him one day. But I never acted on it.

"You didn't fuck him as soon as you turned eighteen?" Mason continued, getting angrier by the second.

"What are you talking about?" I asked, shaking my head. "I didn't do anything with him until recently, until you stopped giving me respect, until you started ogling every other woman who wasn't me."

He smirked cruelly at me. "That's not what I heard."

"And where are you getting this god-awful information from, Mason?" My voice rose with every word, yet I couldn't stop myself. I was so done with his shit. All I wanted to do was get inside the car and drive off, but he was blocking me from the driver's side.

He crossed his arms over his chest and took a step back toward his Mercedes. "A little birdy told me everything you've done with him. You know how bad that's going to look for the both of you when everyone finds out Michael started fucking you at the ripe age of eighteen?"

I clenched my hands into fists. He was pulling shit out of his ass to make me run back to him. He was trying to make me weak, trying to hurt me so I would be his again. And I fucking hated it.

"Do you really think Michael wants you because he loves you? Do you really think you're anything other than a young fuck toy to him? He could get any woman his own age, but he picked you." Mason opened his car door. "Seems kinda fucked up to me."

I yanked open my door and threw my backpack into the passenger side. Damn him and his stupid fucking bullshit. Trying to make me angry. Trying to make me insecure again. I wanted to heal, and this fucker had to—

"You will be mine again," Mason shouted from his car. "All mine."

I scrambled into the car, slammed my door closed, and locked the car about a hundred times, staring through the windshield and holding my fists steady so that I wouldn't do something rash and slam my fists into the steering wheel. Why'd he have to fuck with my life? Why did he even want me back?

# CHAPTER 9

MIA

*I* pulled into work and took a deep breath. After my run-in with Mason, I could barely think straight. I wanted to go home, sink into the bed, and cuddle with Michael. But I still had bills to pay. So, I trudged out of the car, mentally preparing myself for all the half-drunk men from the city tonight, and walked into the bar.

Thankfully, the bar was still fairly quiet when I got in, only a few guys sitting at the counter. I walked to the back, putting on some of my work clothes and throwing my hair into a high pony-tail, and walked back out.

Some guys leaned over the bar—buzzed on a Tuesday night—and eyed me. They looked like they worked down in the city, dressed in suits with *I'm important, and everyone should know it* smirks.

I smiled at them and walked over. "Need anything else?"

"Your number, sweetheart," the blond one said, eyes lingering on my tits.

My cheeks flushed, and I shook my head. "Sorry, I'm taken."

The other one leaned closer to me, moving his fingers against my forearm. "It's just your number. It won't hurt."

"I said no."

I pulled my arm away from them, all my friendliness washing away, and walked toward some other customers at the other side of the bar. But the two guys didn't stop staring at me with that look in their eyes.

Cruel. Disgusting. Terrifying.

Looks that I had seen so many times before when Mason would come home drunk and wanted to have sex with me, when he wouldn't take no for an answer because he always got what he wanted. He was *the man*—or at least he thought he was.

"Come back here, sweetheart," one of the men said again. "Didn't mean to—"

Serena sat down in the seat in front of me, glancing over at the men and pulling me toward her. She pecked me on the cheek. "Hey, babe. How's work?"

To my surprise, the guys took the hint, grabbed their drinks, and walked back to their table. I took a deep breath.

Serena glanced back at them and rolled her eyes. "Surprised they didn't stay and ask for a foursome. Repulsive pigs. Don't know when to take a hint."

After a few moments, she rolled her eyes and glanced back at me, a huge grin crossing her face. "Anyway, I have news!" She clapped her hands together and squealed. "My internship offered me a full-time position!"

I pulled her into a hug from across the counter. "That's great! I'm so excited for you! When do you officially start?"

"Monday, I'll be full-time. Getting paid the big bucks." She giggled. "Well, at least, more than what my internship paid me."

My boss, Sal, walked up from behind Serena and clapped a hand on her shoulder. "New job? That's great news! I've been trying to get Mia out of here forever." He winked, let out a deep chuckle, and pointed to the bottle of whiskey. "Free shots on the house for that."

Serena wiggled her brows and glanced at Sal's departing figure as he disappeared into one of the back rooms. "Think I can get a sugar daddy like Sal?"

I grabbed her a shot and scrunched up my nose. "God, Serena, Sal is like eighty, and gross."

Serena laughed and tipped the glass in my direction. "Hey, a girl's gotta do what a girl's gotta do."

I playfully rolled my eyes and grinned at her. I was so happy that she had gotten a job. Everyone seemed to be moving on with their lives, and I was still stuck in school for another semester. I gulped, everything turning shitty all of a sudden.

"I saw Mason today," I said, gnawing on the inside of my cheek.

Her eyes widened. "What the fuck? Where?"

"When I went to get the car at your house. He was parked out front."

Her hands balled into fists, and I grabbed her shot glass from her hand before she broke it and started bleeding everywhere, like I had a few weeks ago. "Does Michael know?"

I shook my head. I hadn't had time to tell him yet. And the truth was, I didn't want to tell Michael because I didn't want to add to our problems, but I needed to tell him whether I wanted to or not. I didn't want him finding out from Melissa or Mason himself. He needed to hear it from me.

"You'd better tell him!"

"I will. I haven't had a chance to see him after that, and I didn't want to bother him again today."

Serena nodded, then became deathly quiet. Her cheeks tinted pink from the alcohol, and she tugged on a strand of her choco-late-brown hair. "So, speaking of Michael, I'm meeting with Melissa tomorrow, like you suggested."

"You are?"

She nodded and sat back. "It's going to be so damn awkward. I don't know what I'm going to say. But she sounded like she wanted to talk, so I'm going to give it a try. See if Mason's being a dick to her."

"You know she won't say anything," I said, wiping down the counter with a wet rag.

She sighed. "I know, but it's worth a shot."

# CHAPTER 10

MIA

The two guys were back at the bar, pushing their glasses across the counter and asking for another. It took everything in me not to roll my eyes as I grabbed the glasses and poured them another glass of whiskey.

"You sure we can't get your numbers?" the blond asked, leaning over the bar. "We're working down in the city on the towers."

Serena scoffed, totally unimpressed. "And?"

"Thought we could hang out sometime—"

"Mia," someone called from behind them, walking toward me.

I smiled and thanked the heavens that it was Michael, loosening his tie and taking a seat next to Serena. He nodded to the two guys as if he knew them.

Serena nudged Michael. "Your girl is getting hit on by some jackasses."

"Your girl?" one of them asked, backing up and shaking his head. "Sorry, sir. Didn't know she was your girlfriend." They mumbled another few words to him. "We'll see you in the office."

When they walked back to their seats, I raised a brow at Michael. "You know them?"

"Interns," he said. "They work under one of my coworkers."

Serena sipped on her drink and snorted. "They think they're big shots."

Michael grabbed my hand, eyes on me. "How was your day?"

I broke out into a grin, my heart feeling warm.

Serena raised one of her brows and smirked, mouthing to me, *I'm so fucking happy for you.*

As I was about to answer, Sal walked out of the back room, gaze immediately on Michael and me. "I didn't think it was true that you two were together," he said, and I couldn't tell if he was disappointed or not. Unlike usual, his expression was unreadable.

Michael smiled at me, a dimple forming on his right cheek, eyes relaxing. If I wasn't used to that look by now, I'd probably melt in a puddle from it.

Sal leaned in real close to both of us, laying a hand on each of our shoulders. "Please, God, don't tell me that this has been going on for years now."

This was the second time today that I'd heard that we'd been together for years. And while I wanted to wonder where the rumor had started, I didn't have a doubt in my mind that it was Linda, out to make Michael look bad in front of the entire city. I knew she'd do anything to try to redeem herself.

After she and Michael had gotten a divorce, Michael had succeeded in every part of his life. And Linda had fallen into a pit of drugs, disease-ridden men, and alcohol. Or maybe … that was how she always was.

"Only a few months," Michael said, brows furrowing together. He looked from me to Serena to Sal, confusion evident on his face. "Who'd you hear that from?"

"Well," Sal said, scratching the back of his head.

He lifted his eyes to the door behind Michael, and mine followed. Linda walked into the bar.

"Someone is telling everyone in town that Mia broke up your family."

Michael tensed and clenched his jaw. "Fucking Linda," he said through gritted teeth. He shook his head and glanced down at his lap, not even having seen her yet.

When her eyes met mine, her lips curled into a nasty snarl. I gulped.

Damn, why was she here? Why couldn't she leave us alone? Why was it always—

Michael took my hands and squeezed them. "Hey, everything is going to be okay."

"Michael!" Linda shouted from across the room.

Everyone suddenly quieted down, some people glancing over at us. The two goons who had been trying to flirt with me earlier stared intently at her, then back at me.

She looked like she was put together for once in her entire life, but I could tell by the sway in her step that she had been drinking yet again. I had seen that walk one too many times.

She walked toward us, eyes landing on Serena, who sat next to him.

"Fucking two young whores now, Michael? I didn't think you had it in you."

# CHAPTER 11

MIA

*M*ichael tensed and swore under his breath, peering back at Linda, who continued to stumble over to us. Everyone in the entire bar stared over at her, and I couldn't imagine how embarrassing this must've been for Michael.

I grasped his hand tighter, wrapping my fingers around his palm. "Michael, she's trying to get you angry," I whispered to him, but it was too late.

Michael was already fuming at her, his eyes cold, cheeks red with anger. "Are you following us?" he asked through gritted teeth.

"I didn't know you were here," Linda claimed. "I just wanted to come get a drink. This is my favorite place to get drunk, think about better times when my husband wasn't such a prick and didn't prey on little girls."

I glared at her. Michael had said she was his problem, but she was interfering with my life too. She was putting stupid fucking rumors in Mason's head, making him and Melissa think that we'd tarnished their family. And while I trusted Michael to handle this, I couldn't take it anymore.

"It was you, wasn't it?" I asked, drawing her attention away from Michael and to me.

"What was me?" she asked, eyes wild and crazy.

Was she always like this? Always this crazy? This manipulative? This much of a liar? Was that why Michael had finally ended it with her?

My hands balled into fists under the bar, and I realized how stupid I was for not telling Michael that I had run into Mason earlier. I didn't have much time. I had been running late for work, had to speed here to clock in on time.

"Mason," I said, hoping she'd get the damn hint.

Michael tensed and sat up taller. "Mason?"

I clenched my jaw. "Mason came to visit me at Serena's house today. Was standing outside your car, waiting for me ..." I turned back toward her, anger rushing through my veins. I tried to keep my voice quiet, but I couldn't contain my anger any longer. "You've been telling him lies about me and Michael—that I slept with Michael when I turned eighteen."

Linda tilted her head and cackled. "I did no such thing. That boy asked me what happened between us, and I told him the truth."

After taking a deep breath so I didn't punch her straight in the face for wrecking my life, I glanced back at Michael, who looked both hurt and angry.

Guilt washed over me, and I furrowed my brows together and gripped his hand from across the bar. "I refused to let him get near me. I would've called you when it happened, but I was late for work. I'm sorry. I was going to tell you tonight."

Serena nodded at Michael. "She was. She told me."

Linda cackled. "Trouble in paradise?"

She collapsed down onto a barstool next to Serena. Michael

grabbed Serena's arm and pulled her off the stool and away from his ex-wife.

"Anyway, I want something hard."

I pursed my lips together. "I can't serve you."

Her cheeks turned a blazing pink. "I said I wanted a drink."

"And I said I couldn't serve you."

She slammed her palms against the counter. "I want to talk to your manager."

"I am the manager."

"Your boss then." Her voice was tight and laced with anger.

"Linda, don't make a fucking scene," Michael said, anger in his gray eyes.

She turned her head and reached out for him, but he leaned away. "Am I embarrassing you, Michael? Embarrassed of *me* and not how you destroyed my entire life by sleeping with an underage—"

Sal cleared his throat. "I'm going to have to ask you to leave," he said before things could get any worse.

I stared between them, my heart pounding in my chest. Sal only intervened when he thought things could get really bad. There were bar fights every now and then, but not much made Sal this … upset.

"I'm not leaving. I came here for a drink."

"You're harassing my customers. You'll leave, or the police will escort you out," Sal said.

When Linda refused to move, Serena called the police. She shot me a *you did good* look, wiggling her brows and holding up a thumb behind Michael's back. I blew out a deep breath and wiped down the bar.

We waited a good five minutes as Linda continued to make a scene, refused to leave, started insulting all the customers, including the two guys who had tried to hit on us earlier. I rolled my eyes and poured everyone free drinks as Sal said it was to make it up to them.

A police car finally rolled up to the bar, and two cops hopped out of the car. After talking briefly with Sal, the policemen escorted Linda out of the bar and stuck her in the backseat of their cruiser because she was too damn drunk to drive.

I grabbed Michael's hands, squeezing them tightly. All I could read on his face was hate. It wasn't that kind of playful hate. It was the kind felt deep down in your bones, where you hated someone with everything you had because they had ruined and kept ruining your life.

"I'm getting a restraining order against her," he said, shaking his head and glancing back at the police car.

Linda sat in the back of it, staring through the windshield at us with a huge smirk on her face. When he turned back to me, he swept his fingers against my knuckles.

"She's only acting like this because it's you," he said. "Melissa probably told her about us, and now, she's trying to get Melissa back on her side, so she'll hate me too."

"Well, I'll make sure she doesn't," I said.

All those screenshots and messages from Mason weren't for nothing. I'd use them to get her back on his side, so she knew Mason was bad for her.

"Mason?" Michael asked. He stayed quiet for a few moments, then grasped my hands tighter, as if I'd leave him. "Be honest with me, Mia … do you still love him? Is that why you didn't tell me about him when it happened?"

I shook my head. "No, of course not."

Michael had proven to me over and over and over again that he wouldn't leave me when times got tough. But … the past had a stupid fucking way of screwing you up for the future.

No matter how deep I buried it, some part of me thought I wasn't good enough for Michael. I hadn't been good enough for Dad. I hadn't been good enough for Mason. Why did I think I deserved someone as good as Michael?

But before I could think the worst, I pushed away those nasty thoughts. Michael loved me, had told me that he wanted me more than anything, that he wanted to spend his life with me. And I wanted to spend my life with him too.

"I …" I glanced down at the bar and frowned. "Michael, I love you more than anyone. I'm just dealing with my insecurities right now, thinking about shit that I know I shouldn't. It's difficult for me to open up about everything."

He gently seized my chin and forced me to glance up at him. "You know I got you, right?"

I smiled and leaned across the bar. "As long as it's forever."

"Forever, Mia."

# CHAPTER 12

MIA

*A*fter last night, I hadn't been able to stop thinking about what had happened. No matter how much I tried to ignore Linda's rumors, they were starting to drip into other aspects of my life. And I needed to talk to someone.

Mom was out of the picture, as I didn't want to worry her right now.

Serena had already heard it all.

Michael was stressed out.

So, I only had one more option left. I sat in my psychology class, waiting patiently for it to end. It was three minutes until noon, and students were already packing up to leave. I pulled out my phone and messaged Serena, unsure if I'd see her before she talked to Melissa.

**Me: Good luck tonight. xx Please talk some sense into Melissa.**

She responded almost immediately.

**Serena: Thanks. Gonna need it.**

When Dr. Xiao dismissed everyone, I lingered behind and walked up to her desk. She smiled at me and sat down.

"I've been waiting for this," she said, nodding to a chair in front of her. "Take a seat."

I hesitantly sat down, my knees bouncing wildly, and opened my mouth to speak, but nothing would come out. What was I supposed to say? I didn't want things to get even worse with these rumors.

But Dr. Xiao didn't say a word. She sipped on her coffee and urged me to say something.

I clasped my hands together and looked at the ground. "I'm sure you've heard the rumors going around our town."

She furrowed her brows. "No, I haven't."

"About Michael Bryne?" I asked quietly.

"Michael Bryne? He's an architect, correct, working on the towers down in the city?"

I hesitantly nodded and took a deep breath. It didn't seem like she knew what I was talking about at all, which made me feel so much better. At least we weren't the talk of the town yet. Some people didn't know.

"Yes ... and I'm dating him." I paused for a moment, letting my emotions overtake me. "We have a huge age gap between us, and his ex-wife is becoming a burden, spreading rumors about us, hurting our relationship ..." Tears welled up in my eyes. It felt so good to get this out to someone I could trust.

She moved from behind her desk toward me. "Mia—"

"And he's my ex–best friend's dad," I said, unable to hold myself back. "And my mom can't form new memories. My ex-boyfriend cheated on me with my best friend. My life is a mess, Dr. Xiao."

Her brown eyes widened, and she pulled me into a tight hug. "Mia, I had no idea." She held me for a few moments, and then she pulled back and smiled at me. "If it makes you feel any better, I've heard my fair share of rumors about my relationship. My

49

husband's fifteen years older than me, and so many people hated it. When we first started dating, my parents refused to meet him and even stopped talking to me for the longest time."

She pushed a strand of hair from my face. "But when you're in love, you're in love." She let out a sigh. "You can't help it, and you can't stop it. If it's true and real … don't mind the rumors. Who cares? You know what's real, what's true. Don't let small minds mess with it."

I nodded and gave her a small smile back. "Thank you," I whispered.

She shrugged her shoulders and patted my knee. "I know you're going through a lot right now, but things will get better. Trust in yourself and your relationship. It'll be all right."

And in that moment, I had hope. Hope that one day, these rumors would die off. Hope that one day, I'd finally have that happily ever after with Michael. Hope that Linda would stop ruining everything Michael had tried so hard to achieve.

# CHAPTER 13

MICHAEL

"*M*ichael," Mia mumbled into the pillow, her voice light with laughter.

I snaked my hand around her waist and rubbed the front of her underwear with my fingers. They were soaked, drenched, just wanting to be ripped off. She let out another laugh and arched her back, rubbing her ass against my dick.

"We don't have enough time."

I pressed my lips on her neck, leaving a trail of kisses down to her shoulder. The morning sunlight flooded into our bedroom through the window. I pulled her onto her back, my lips brushing down her chest to her lacy panties. My cock pulsing and aching to be inside of her. But she was right. We didn't have enough time.

So, instead, I spread her legs, rested her thighs on my shoulders, hooked one finger into her underwear, and pulled it to the side. My mouth found her clit, my fingers pushing into her tight pussy.

She thrust her hand into my hair and tugged. "Oh God ..." she whimpered.

I added another finger, pumping them faster into her as I flicked my tongue against her clit.

"More. Faster. Don't stop."

I pressed my cock into the mattress, imagining how good it'd feel to be inside of my girlfriend's wet pussy, how easily it'd slide right in, how deep and warm it'd be inside, and groaned against her.

She moved her hips back and forth, but I held her still and flicked my tongue against her clit. God, I loved the way her body reacted to me. Since the first night we'd spent together, I couldn't get enough of her. I wanted as much as I could get, wanted to taste her whenever I had the chance, to fill her, to make her feel so good that she couldn't stop herself from screaming my name.

Her legs trembled against my shoulders. My fingers pumped in and out of her, my tongue moving effortlessly against her clit. My cock was so fucking stiff from me watching her move.

She stared down at me, lips parted and eyes glazed over with lust. I stuck my other fingers into her mouth and watched her suck them as if she were sucking my dick.

When she tightened around me, I curled my fingers inside of her, letting my thumb hit her clit. She screamed out my name, her body trembling, her pussy pulsing over and over on me. Fuck, she always looked so damn sexy when she came this hard for me.

I ground my hips into the bed and pulled my fingers out of her. She took a deep breath, pressed a kiss on my lips, and disappeared into our bathroom for a quick shower. I rested against the bed, breathing heavily, my hand stroking my cock through my briefs. I'd wait to come later when we had more time and when I was inside of her.

Mia took a quick five minutes, throwing herself together—the fastest I'd ever seen a woman get ready. It took a good hour for

Melissa and even longer for Linda to do anything. She gave me a kiss and left for the hospital.

After my shower, I readjusted my tie in the mirror, grabbed my keys and wallet, and opened the front door to go to work. I stopped dead in my tracks when I saw Melissa walking up the sidewalk toward me.

I glanced around, looking for any sign of Linda but not finding any. While I didn't want to be late for work, I couldn't pass up this opportunity to try to talk some sense into Melissa about Mason.

When she reached me, she frowned. "You're about to head to work, aren't you?"

I opened the door wider and let my briefcase slip off my shoulder and onto the ground. Mia wanted me to repatch things with Melissa, was willing to deal with Mason's stupid fucking messages. And I wanted to talk. We had never spent this much time apart, and I hated it.

"I have time."

She awkwardly stepped into the house and frowned at Mia's flip-flops by the front door. "So," Melissa said, walking up the stairs and glancing around the house, as if she expected it to look any different, "how's everything going?"

"Are you asking how I am or how things are with Mia?" I asked, following her to the kitchen.

After eyeing a banana on the counter, she sat down at the kitchen table.

I placed the banana on the table in front of her and nodded toward it. "Eat it."

She peeled it and took a deep breath. "Both."

I leaned against the counter, fingers gripping the edges. "Mia and I are doing really good." I parted my lips, unsure if I should say what I wanted to say next, but I did anyway because Melissa would find out sooner or later. "We're serious about our relationship, Melissa. *I'm* more serious than I have been with any other woman."

Melissa stayed quiet. She didn't want to hear this, but she needed to.

"I plan to spend the rest of my life with her."

Melissa's eyes widened, yet she still didn't say anything.

"But I'm not going to move forward with her until you and I are good," I said, my chest tightening up. "Because it sucks around here, not getting to see or talk to you."

She frowned and stared at the ground. She looked like she wanted to say something, and I wanted to beg her to get on with it, to tell me that she missed me too, to tell me that she had remorse—even the slightest bit—for what she'd done.

But instead of apologizing, she asked, "You love her a lot, don't you?"

"Yes," I said. "But I love you too. You're always going to be my girl, Melissa. Just because I'm dating someone doesn't mean that I'm not going to treat you how you deserve. But you being my daughter doesn't mean I'm always going to go easy on you either. I want you to grow, be the person, student, worker I know you can be."

She gulped and threw the banana peel in the garbage, her eyes filling with tears. She fiddled with her fingers and looked down at her phone. Mason's name flashed on the screen, and Melissa stood. "I have to go."

She hurried to the door, and I followed her.

"Melissa, wait. Please don't go back to him. He's no good for you."

She opened the front door and looked back at me. "I miss you, Dad." Then, she walked right out and to her car without saying anything else.

I stared at her departing car from the doorway and frowned at it, my throat closing up.

"I miss you too," I whispered to myself, everything hurting.

# CHAPTER 14

MIA

St. Barbars Assisted Living looked busy this morning, cars parked in almost every spot, patients walking around the front of the building with nurses and family members. My phone buzzed from the passenger seat, Michael's name flashing on the screen.

**Michael: Melissa stopped over.**

I stared down at the phone with wide eyes. Serena must've talked some sense into her yesterday. At least, I hoped she had. I didn't want Melissa to have come over, yelling at Michael or something.

**Me: She did? What'd she say?**

**Michael: Not much.**

A few moments passed.

**Michael: That she missed me.**

My heart ached, my chest tightening. I frowned and tried to bite back the tears. Even over text, I could tell how much those few words meant to him. He and Melissa might've been going through a rough patch right now … but they still missed each other. And I wished that I had something like that with Dad.

But he was an asshole who didn't give a single fuck about me.

**Me: That's great! Are you talking now?**

I had to wait a few moments for his reply.

**Michael: I'm not sure. I hope so. I miss her too.**

**Michael: I have to go. See you when I get home tonight.**

I pushed my phone into my pocket and grabbed my coffee, walking toward the entrance of the building. Part of me wished I hadn't tarnished their relationship, but I didn't want to apologize for falling for Michael. He was the best thing to ever happen to me, and I wouldn't trade him for the entire world.

Just as I walked into the lobby, my phone buzzed again. This time, it was Serena.

**Serena: Meet me at Dunkin' downtown at four. I have some news about Melissa.**

"Mia, isn't it?" the receptionist asked.

I put my phone away for good and smiled at her. It was the same woman there as last time, the one who had thought I was Michael's daughter.

She gave me a tense smile. "No Michael today?"

"He's working," I said awkwardly, signing my name into their sign-in notebook.

Before I let go of the pen, the woman grabbed my wrist. "Are you okay?" she asked, voice quiet. I tried to pull my hand away, but she held me tighter. "You can tell me if something is wrong. I can help you."

I furrowed my brows and yanked my hand away, smoothing out my skirt. "I'm fine. Why?"

"Michael … I thought he was a nice guy but …" She set her lips in a tight line. "Oh, never mind. It's nothing. Probably just some rumors going around town." She eyed her computer and smiled. "Your mother is down the hall."

But I didn't move. I stayed there, glued to the spot. First, it was Mason, and now, it was this woman at the goddamn assisted living home, telling me these rumors about Michael.

"What rumors?"

Her cheeks flushed. "Nothing. Maybe I'm mistaken."

"What rumors?" I asked through gritted teeth. I knew exactly what rumors she was talking about, yet I needed to hear how much Linda had screwed things for us.

She gulped and drew her tongue across her teeth. "Just that …" She looked everywhere, except at me. "That he took advantage of you when you were younger and ruined his and his wife's relationship."

I flared my nostrils.

"If he took advantage of you when you were younger, that isn't love, and I think you should—"

I slammed my palm down on the counter. "Not that it is any of your business, but our relationship is and has always been completely consensual and legal. I didn't wreck anyone's relationship. I didn't do anything with him before I was eighteen." My gaze flickered to her name tag. "Don't believe all the rumors you hear, *Carol*."

And with that, I walked right out of the lobby, feeling everyone's eyes burn into my back. I tried to contain my anger, but when I reached Mom's door, I had to take a deep breath. I wouldn't let Linda destroy my relationship. Never in a million years.

*Michael is mine now. Not yours, Linda, you bitch.*

Mom sat on her bed, staring happily out the window at the bird feeder Michael and I had gotten her the other day. There was a bluebird perched on a wooden stick, munching on some seeds.

"Sweetheart," Mom said. "How are you?"

"Doing good, Mom," I said, sitting on the side of her bed.

"What arc you up to this weekend?"

"I'm going to Michael's work party," I said.

"Work party?" she asked. "Things must be getting pretty serious between you and him."

She raised a brow at me, and I smiled back. I hoped she'd get her memories back soon. It was difficult on me; it must've been even more difficult on her.

I rested my head against her shoulder and talked to her about Linda and the mess she'd gotten us into. Mom nodded along, giving me her advice to ignore the rumors—no matter how hard they got, those rumors were what people talked about because their lives were boring and had nothing better to chat about.

After a couple hours, James showed up and sat in his usual chair, watching the birds. I left them alone because I definitely didn't want to interfere with whatever they did at this assisted living center together.

But instead of leaving, I walked down the hall toward Michael's father's room. I knocked on the door and didn't see Michael's father inside of the room. A nurse smiled at me.

"Looking for Mr. Bryne?" She nodded toward the garden. "A nurse took him out there a while ago."

After I thanked her, I walked out into the garden and inhaled the morning scent. Michael's father sat in a wheelchair in front of a small pond, the sun hitting his face. I took a deep breath and walked over to him, not knowing what I was going to say.

But I wanted to talk to him.

"Mia," Mr. Bryne said, smiling at me. "How are you?"

# CHAPTER 15

MIA

*J* glanced at the time on my phone and walked into Dunkin', scanning the room to see if Serena was here yet. When I didn't see her, I grabbed two coffees from the barista and found a table for us.

My talk with Mr. Bryne had taken longer than I'd expected it to. I planned to be there for fifteen minutes at the most. Though it might've been awkward between us, Mr. Bryne could talk. I'd ended up leaving the assisted living center at two p.m.—just enough time to gather my things back at home and get here.

We'd talked about everything we could. He told me embarrassing stories of Michael when he was younger and gave me some pictures from a photo album of Michael when he was in college. And, Lord, when I saw those pictures, I nearly died. I'd snagged myself a hottie.

I grinned and sat back in the chair, peeling my orange. And somehow, speaking to Michael's father had made this whole thing—these rumors, Linda, our age difference—less awkward for me. Mr. Bryne hadn't treated me any differently. He smiled and laughed and didn't show any tinge of judgment in his eyes.

It'd felt good.

Serena walked through the door, spotted me, and immediately made a beeline for the table. There were dark bags under her eyes, and she yawned when she sat down in front of me. I pushed her a coffee, which she chugged.

"So?" I asked, brow raised. "How'd it go?"

Before Serena even said two words, she finished the coffee, leaned back, and groaned. "I tried. I really tried. I didn't know if I got through to her at all though. She didn't believe me when I told her that Mason had been texting you or that he met up with you the other day."

"Did she not believe you or not want to believe you?" I asked. Because those were two totally different things.

I'd wanted to believe that Mason was good for me. I'd wanted to believe that he really loved me, that I could spend the rest of my life with him, that the sex would get better ... but deep down, I had known otherwise.

She frowned. "Give me the screenshots," she said to me, leaning over the table and kicking her legs back and forth. "I'll send them to her as proof, but I don't know if she'll take them."

I scrolled through my endless messages from him, taking screenshots of them all and sending them over to Serena. Her phone kept buzzing on the table, her eyes widening as she looked at the messages.

"Damn, he's desperate. Who sends that many messages without a response?"

Mason had ... when he realized that I wasn't the same girl he could abuse anymore.

"How is she?" I asked, my stomach tightening as I prepared for the answer. I didn't know what I expected Serena to say or if I expected her to say anything, but something told me that I should be worried.

"She says that she's not being hurt by him in any way, but I don't believe it." She peered out the window. "I think there's more to it. She looks tired, sad. But maybe that's because she misses her father ... I don't know."

"Well, she did go see him this morning," I said. I wished she'd see him more often even if I never saw her. I didn't mind that. All I wanted was for them to have a good, strong relationship.

"Speaking of Michael, I'm going to see his work friends tonight," I said, dread scratching at the inside of my stomach. After my little run-in with the receptionist earlier at the assisted living center, I felt like shit about tonight.

She wiggled her brows. "Looks like you and he are getting very serious."

I smiled and leaned back in the seat. "Yeah ... he told me he wanted to spend his life with me."

Serena nearly choked on her coffee. "Nuh-uh."

"Yes-huh."

She smacked the table with her palm and jumped out of her seat. "Oh my gosh. Girl, you know what I hear?!"

I glanced around. "Coffee being brewed?"

After playfully slapping my arm, she sat back down, humming the "Bridal Chorus."

I scrunched up my nose and shook my head. "No, he wouldn't," I said, but my stomach was fluttering with butterflies. "Not so soon. I mean ..."

"You've been dating for more than a few months, sure. But he's been with you through the hardest time of your entire life. He stayed with you at the hospital for weeks. He sacrificed his nights, told you he loves you." Serena shook her head. "And now, he tells you he wants to spend his life with you, and you don't think he wants to marry you?"

Michael and I getting married? I gulped. I hadn't even thought about it yet. Did he want to marry me? His relationship with

Melissa was screwed up. If we got married now … I didn't know if it'd ever be repaired.

"You think so?" I gnawed on the inside of my cheek, nerves running through me.

Serena raised a brow at me. "No, I think he's going to dump you," she said sarcastically. But then she leaned closer to me and took my hands. "I'm just kidding. What would you say if he asked?"

I parted my lips and pressed them back together. God, I would say yes a million times. But my better judgment would tell me to wait, that Melissa needed to be okay with this first, that she needed help even though she might not ask for it.

"I would say … yes."

# CHAPTER 16

MIA

"It's just a work party, Mia." Michael placed his hand on my lower back, guiding me down the sidewalk toward Silver's Steakhouse, a large bar where companies reserved space to host work parties.

Cars and buses raced down the street beside us, and the towers stood monstrously all the way across the city.

I nodded and pretended like I was fine.

I wasn't nervous at all.

Nah. Nope. Definitely not me.

*I am going to go in there and rock it.* Not.

When Michael opened the door, I stopped dead in my tracks and stared at all the people. Oh God, there were so many damn people here. How was I going to talk to any of them? I could barely talk to the server at Dunkin' earlier.

"You're fine," Michael said, pressing a kiss on my cheek. He grabbed my hand and led me directly to the bar, giving me a glass of white wine and telling me to relax again.

The bartender smiled and poured more than enough wine for me, filling it up more than he had with others. After throwing me a smile, he set the glass in front of me. "Looks like you need it."

I took a huge gulp from it and breathed deeply. Was I fine? No. Was I going to stay for Michael? Of course.

Dressed in a black suit and tie, Michael smiled down at me. "You better?"

"Yes," I said, patting his chest. "I'm fine."

No, I really wasn't.

But I didn't have time to tell Michael that because he led me toward some people near the other side of the bar. My heart pounded against my chest. Was I overreacting? Probably, but making friends wasn't my strong suit. I had been friends with the same five people: Melissa, Serena, Damien, Mason, and Victor since high school, and now, I was out in the real world, about to chat with people I hadn't met before, wondering if they were looking at me strangely because I was so young or because I looked like I was about to have a stroke.

When we approached them, they all seemed to quiet down.

One of the men held out his hand for Michael to shake. "Michael, glad you could make it." He glanced over at me. "Is this Mia?"

Michael flashed him that devilishly handsome smile. "Yes, this is Mia."

I gave them my best smile, trying to hide the fact that my stomach was in knots. The women glanced over at me, giving me tight smiles, and the guys' eyes lingered for a moment more than I was comfortable with.

Almost immediately, Michael fell into an easy conversation with them, chatting about the towers, new projects they'd be working on soon, the interns from the bar. I squeezed Michael's hand tightly and took another sip of my wine.

I'd prepared all day for this dinner party, yet here I was, standing with Michael, watching him talk so effortlessly with everyone. And I was a mess. There was a thin layer of sweat coating my lower back, my heart was racing every time someone looked at me for more than a few moments, and I felt like I was about to have a panic attack.

A strand of Michael's dark hair curled over his forehead, his sparkling gray eyes lighting up the damn room. He was such a smooth talker; he knew exactly what to say and when to say it. How to get a rise out of someone. How to make someone—me—blush. How to get people excited to start on another project.

I took one more sip of my wine, the taste more bitter than usual, and put it down on the table. I needed to get some air, away from these people.

Michael glanced over at me, brow raised. "You don't like it? I can get you something else."

"I'm going to get some water," I said, patting his shoulder. "I'll be back." I walked over to the bar, trying to ignore the stares from some of the older women, and smiled at the bartender.

He finished making a white sangria for someone by plopping an orange slice into the wineglass. My stomach growled at the mere sight of it, and I licked my dry lips. He slid the glass to one of Michael's colleagues and walked over to me.

"Back for another?" he asked, smiling.

"Water."

"Water." He placed a glass on the counter and filled it nearly to the brim with water.

He pushed the glass toward me, but I lingered near the bar, eyeing the pre-sliced oranges in a small container.

"Can I have one too?"

He raised a brow and chuckled. "An orange?"

My stomach growled, and I nodded. "Please."

After pulling one out and dropping it into my water, he smiled. "Anything for you."

I smiled back and was about to turn back around, but he grabbed my wrist.

"Hey, don't sweat it." He nodded back to the group Michael was with. "They're just people. You don't have to look like you're about to faint around them."

"And what if I am?"

He wiped the bar down with a rag. "You won't."

"They seem very judgy."

"Many businesspeople here are. They're just jealous. Don't let them get to you."

After nodding and thanking him, I turned back around and plucked the orange right out of the glass, sucking it into my mouth and moaning quietly to myself. I didn't know what kind of addictive shit they put in these here, but it tasted good tonight.

I took my time walking back to Michael, not wanting to go back to those judgmental stares. But we were here for him, and I was going to suck it up, no matter how much I wished I'd stayed home by myself.

Michael wanted me here. Michael made me face my fears. Michael was my man. And I'd support him, no matter what. But I had a feeling in the pit of my stomach that this night was about to get a whole lot worse.

# CHAPTER 17

MIA

*A*fter a few hours of talking with his coworkers, Michael grabbed my hand and led me toward a door near the side of the bar. Before he pulled me out of it, he glanced back to make sure nobody was watching, then pulled me down the hall toward the elevators. "I want to show you something."

As soon as we stepped onto the elevator, I released all the stress and anxiety in a huge sigh. God, it had been difficult to keep up tonight. I'd tried talking to some of his coworkers, striking up some conversation about something. But it was difficult for me to relate to any of them. I was still in college, working on getting my bachelor's, while most of them had been working for the past twenty years at least.

Michael tapped Button 30 in the elevator and grabbed my hand. When the elevator doors opened, we were on top of the damn building.

Wind chilled my skin, and I walked outside. There was a large garden with all different types of flowers, like its own little jungle. I grinned. This was breathtaking and exactly what I needed.

I walked around the flowers, letting my fingers brush against the petals, and Michael followed after me. We weaved our way through the makeshift garden until we came to the end, where there were some benches secured into the building near the edge.

After wandering toward the edge, I glanced down at the tiny cars below. We were only thirty stories in the air, but the sight was beyond beautiful. I took in a deep breath, wanting to savor this moment forever.

Michael rested his hands on the railing on either side of me. "Do you like it?" he asked, nose grazing against my ear.

I shivered in delight and smiled at the sparkling city lights. He grinded into me from behind, and I closed my eyes, knowing exactly what he wanted.

"Michael," I whispered. "We can't ... not here."

"Pull up the back of your dress."

I glanced back through the garden. "Michael, what if someone comes up here and sees us?"

He pressed into me from behind, making me feel his cock. I bit back a moan and pushed back into him, letting his dick rub against my ass. God, this was what I needed right now. This party was stressing me out.

"Pull up your dress, Mia. I won't ask again."

I gulped and pulled up the back of my dress, feeling the warmth pool between my legs.

Michael slapped my backside, grabbing a cheek in his hand. "Arch your back. Let me see it."

After sucking in a deep breath, I arched my back. He drew a finger against my folds and pushed one into my entrance. My pussy pulsed around it, and I bit my lip to hold in a moan.

"Please, Michael, give me more."

He pushed another finger into me, ramming them in and out,

making my pussy make sloppy, wet sounds for him. He wrapped one hand around the front of my throat and leaned over me, pressing his hardness against me.

"More," I breathed. "Please, I need more."

I squeezed my eyes shut and reached behind me to stroke his cock. Tension was building higher and higher in my pussy. I was seconds away from—

"Don't come until I'm inside of you, Mia."

My body shuddered against him, my mind foggy with pleasure. I tried to suppress the pressure pushing me higher and higher to the edge. I fumbled with his zipper with one hand and used my other hand to grip on to the ledge.

God, this was exhilarating.

He pulled his fingers out of me and freed his cock, pushing the head against my entrance and stroking himself quickly.

I pushed my hips back. "Please, give it to me."

He gripped my waist and shoved his cock deep into my pussy. I clenched around him, adjusting to his size. He pushed himself even deeper, and I bit my lip to hold in my moan.

He wrapped his hand around the front of my throat, holding me close to him, nose against my ear, breath warming my neck. "Look at it, Mia."

I stared down at the city, my heart racing in my chest. It was beautiful. Absolutely beautiful.

He pumped into me from behind and lightly bit my exposed neck. "You look stunning tonight."

My breasts bounced lightly against the railing, my nipples stiffening under my dress. One of his arms slipped around my hip, and he rubbed my clit, sending more heat to my core.

"Please, Michael, give me more," I breathed out, tightening my pussy around him.

He pressed kisses up and down the column of my neck and pounded faster.

I placed my palms on the ledge, squeezing it and staring down at the city. He lifted one of my legs into the air, giving himself better access to plunge deeper into me, and pulled me against him and squeezed lightly.

"You're doing amazing tonight," he praised.

My pussy pulsed on him. He continued to pound into me, his thrusts becoming faster, as his fingers moved in furious circles around my clit. The force pushed me higher and higher.

"Do you want a reward?"

Lord, I wasn't going to last that long.

"Yes, please," I breathed out, trying to hold myself together for a bit longer.

"Tell me where and when you want my cum, Mia," he murmured against me.

"Inside of me …" My leg posted on the ground buckled. "Please, now," I moaned as I came on his cock. I grasped on to the railing for dear life and came so much harder and so much longer than last time, my whole body tingling.

Michael groaned against me and pulled out of me, pushing some hair behind my ear. Well, that was one way to get me to want to come out with him and his coworkers more often. I wasn't going to be as reluctant next time if he rewarded me like this afterward.

After we snuck back into the party, I excused myself to use the restroom. I needed to cool off after that and catch my breath. That had to be some of the most exhilarating sex I had ever had. Who else could say they snuck away from a work party and fucked on top of a building in the middle of summer?

When I finished my business and calmed down, I readied myself for the rest of this night and walked out of the restroom. I was going to make this night the best it could—

Before I turned a corner, I heard Michael's name being used in a conversation behind the door. It sounded like two male coworkers, laughing to themselves. And then one of the men said something that made me cut like a knife in the heart.

"Props to Michael. He's got a piece of fresh young pussy, and he knows it."

# CHAPTER 18

MICHAEL

*M*ia had been nervous all night. For a moment, I saw her loosen up when she went to the bar and chatted with the bartender, who looked to be around her age. I didn't know what she was so worried about though. She had done wonderful tonight.

After she disappeared into the restroom, I waited at a table for her to come back, so we could leave. I sipped on the last of my wine and nodded to Jim, who was talking to a group of the male architects about another project we'd be starting soon.

"So, Michael," Jim said, turning the conversation toward me. He raised his brows. "Mia?"

I nodded and gave him a tight smile, hoping we hadn't given too much away when we disappeared for a solid twenty minutes. "She's amazing," I said, glancing back at the restroom. *Where is she?*

"I bet she is."

Some of the interns chuckled, but I didn't because there wasn't anything to laugh about.

"Been going on for a while, huh?" he asked.

One of the younger interns from the other night at Sal's bar nudged him. "Bagged her at eighteen." He whistled, as if he was impressed, and chuckled. "Got a nice set of tits too."

The guys started laughing, but I felt bitter disgust deep in my bones. Spreading rumors and lies to act cool in front of the group. How mature.

"No," I said, strong and clear so they completely understood me. I tried hard not to let it affect me, to stay calm, to not clench my jaw so tightly. "She's twenty-two. Young, but not that young."

"Still though," another one of the guys said, suggestively raising his brows, "you scored with her."

It was shit-talking, just *what guys did*, but it didn't fly with me. To even hear them talk about Mia like she was nothing but a fuck toy disgusted me. She was more than that, had always been more than that. It'd started physical, but even then, she hadn't been an object.

"I'd appreciate it if you respected her," I said, placing my drink down on the table and glancing back to the restrooms.

Mia caught my eye from across the room, her face as pale as a ghost.

"She's not an object. She's my girlfriend," I said.

Jim nudged me. "Don't take it so personal. You know how it is."

I ground my teeth together and stared over at them. "And how is it?"

He paused and looked away, tilting his head, as if he didn't know how to respond to that without sounding disrespectful. "Just locker-room talk."

My hands balled into fists, and I willed myself not to make a bigger scene. This was what Mia had been worried about even though I'd told her not to worry one bit. She had known this would happen, and I'd brushed it off as if it were nothing.

Mia's gaze met mine, and a pained expression crossed her face. Something had happened. Something that I knew I wouldn't like. I wanted to leave with her now, but I wanted them to know not to fucking treat her like she was good for nothing but sex.

I didn't know how any of these guys had relationships while disrespecting women this much.

"I don't give a damn if it's locker-room talk. It's disgusting," I said through gritted teeth. I wanted to say more, but Mia looked beyond stressed. So, I grabbed my suit jacket and swung it over my shoulder. "I have to go."

Without listening to another word from them, I hurried toward Mia. She faked a smile, pretending as if everything were okay. But as soon as I grabbed her hand, her smile faltered, and she dropped the act.

"I'm sorry for ruining the night"—she nodded toward the door—"but can we go? I ... I don't want to make you leave if you don't want to leave, but ..." She glanced back at the way she had come and gulped, a solemn expression crossing her face. "But I want to go home. I don't feel comfortable here."

I gently grasped the back of her neck and pulled her closer, pressing a kiss on her forehead. "You didn't ruin the night."

I grabbed her hand and walked with her toward the exit. Because if I asked her what had happened while she was in the restroom while I was still here, I might lose it.

When we walked into the night, a breeze chilling my exposed skin, I interlocked my fingers with hers. "Now, tell me what happened."

# CHAPTER 19

MIA

*M*aybe it was all the stress getting to me or the rumors or work. But after hearing his work colleagues talk as if I were some fuck toy to Michael, I felt like shit. I'd tried to not let it get to me, but as I walked through the crowd of people, I had seen those looks. Some from the older females, giving me nasty stares. Some from the guys—both old and young—ogling me.

Michael placed his hand on my lower back and guided me down the sidewalk toward the parking garage. "What happened?" he urged again when I didn't respond the first time.

"Nothing," I said, placing a hand on my stomach. "I just don't feel too good. That wine made my stomach hurt." It wasn't a lie. I couldn't finish the glass like usual. I just … it was disgusting for some reason tonight.

He grimaced like he didn't believe me and opened the passenger door for me. I scooted into the car and stared out the windshield. I licked my dry lips, my knees bouncing wildly. He sat next to me and glanced over.

By the look on his face, I could tell that he wanted to say something, that something had happened with him too. But instead of saying anything, he started the car and drove us home. It was a short, quiet ride. I leaned my head against the seat and watched the buildings turn into trees and the bright city skyline be replaced by the natural light of the moon and stars.

When he pulled into the driveway, he shut off the car and turned to face me. "What happened?" he asked again, pushing a strand of hair from my face.

My lips quivered, and I begged myself to not let any tears fall, but one did.

"Am I some fresh young pussy to you?" My words came out weak and frail, and I felt so stupid as soon as they left my mouth.

But, damn, did rumors really get to me. That was what they did. They tore you down until you started to believe them yourself despite knowing better.

Michael got quiet, hand tightening on my thigh. "Who said that to you?"

I gulped and turned to him, eyes glossy. "Am I?" I asked, words no higher than a whisper.

"Of course you're not," he said, grasping my chin and forcing me to stare into his eyes. "You should know better than to ask that. I love you more than anything. I have never and would never treat you as an object."

My frown deepened. "I know."

At that moment, so much guilt washed over me, and I thought about breaking up with Michael. Not because he was a bad guy. Not because he had done something wrong. Not because I didn't love him. But because … I was so fucked up. I had so many insecurities that I hadn't even known existed, and I wanted to work on myself to be a better me, so I didn't annoy Michael or fuck him up too.

"If you know, then why are you asking?"

My heart hammered against my chest. "Can I be honest with you?"

He gave me a hard *you know you can* stare. "What is it?"

"I love you so fucking much. It scares me. I think that one day, you'll see how insecure I am and want to leave me. I feel like I'm not good enough for you even though you tell me I am every day. I'm scared of loving you this much, Michael. I … I'm so fucked up from my last relationships. I don't want to fuck you up too."

He tilted his head. "You think I'm not fucked up? Do you think it didn't take me years to heal from Linda? I know how you're feeling. I know you feel desperate and alone, afraid that I'm going to leave you because you think you're worthless. It's a shitty feeling."

There was silence for a few moments, and I gathered all my courage to speak. "What happened with Linda? I know she's kind of … well, you know. But why'd you really get a divorce?" I asked, my voice barely above a whisper.

His entire body tensed, and he pulled away from me, staring out the windshield at the white wooden fence in front of us. "We weren't the best kids in school, got in trouble often, shit like that. We were young when she got pregnant. Still in high school, had our entire lives ahead of us, and didn't know how we were going to raise a kid. When Melissa was born, I dedicated my time to her and to giving her a better life. I went to college, and Linda stayed home and turned to alcohol."

He took a deep breath. "It wasn't until five years in that I admitted to myself that she had a problem. I thought I could fix it. I let her take her anger out on me, so she wouldn't yell at Melissa. I let her talk down to me, tell me I wasn't good enough, verbally abuse me … but I stayed because I didn't want Melissa to come from a broken home. She was still young, and at the time, Linda still cared about her.

"But as time went on … she slipped deeper into alcohol.

Started doing drugs. Took our money we'd saved for Melissa's college and gambled it away. It was bad, and I couldn't take it anymore. She didn't care about Melissa, so I divorced her."

He tightened his grip on the steering wheel. "I had fallen out of love with her within the first five years, but I'd stayed because I wanted Melissa to feel loved. I should've left with her. I shouldn't have kept Melissa in that environment where that kind of abuse was the norm. If I had a second chance, I'd do it differently."

There was so much hurt and anguish in his voice. I rested my hand on his thigh and squeezed, showing him that I still loved him, no matter what had happened. I didn't know what to say though; it all brought back bad memories of Dad.

"All I wanted to do was hurt people like Linda hurt me. I self-sabotaged all my relationships, all the flings I had with other women after her. Didn't trust them not to hurt me. Didn't think that anyone could really love me for me. I thought they were all like her ..."

"And then?"

"And then I met Julie," he said, one hand on the steering wheel.

Something tugged in my heart, and I knew I could never break up with him. I couldn't bear to have him with anyone else. This man was everything to me, and he was mine. I'd have to work on myself by myself, but I could still love Michael. It would take time to heal.

"She wasn't my type, but she was sweet. I started to trust again." He blew a deep breath out of his nose, as if he was reminiscing on old times, and frowned. "But I wasn't attracted to her. She was nice, cared about me, but ... I didn't love her. I couldn't love her. Something inside of me wouldn't let me."

He clutched my knee, moonlight bouncing off his face. I watched him carefully, feeling so good myself, just hearing that Michael understood me. He had been through this before. He had felt how I felt, knew exactly how difficult it was to look in the mirror and feel nothing but hurt and pain.

"And then I met you," he said, smiling. "Well … I had met you before, but when I saw you at the house with Mason, the way he treated you … I couldn't *not* show you that there was something more."

"You wanted to be my savior?"

"No," he said. "I just didn't want you to drown in a loveless relationship."

My insides felt warm. "When did you know you were in love with me?"

The question took him by surprise. He raised his brows, eyes lighting up the entire car. "When did I know I was in love with you?" He contemplated for a few moments, then smiled. "It was one night we were at the hospital. We were eating dinner. It was raining outside. You were watching the raindrops roll down the window. You looked over at me with a soft smile, and I knew."

He cupped my face gently and lifted it. "It's going to take time … I know it is. But I'm not going anywhere. I promised you forever, and I mean forever."

# CHAPTER 20

MIA

*T*he next morning, my stomach felt like it was about to burst. I tore the blankets off of me and stumbled out of bed toward our bathroom, doubling over the toilet and grasping on to the seat.

*Please, don't be all that wine. Please, don't be all the wine. Anything but that wine.*

"Mia," Michael said, his voice groggy with sleep. "What's going on? Are you okay?"

I heaved into the toilet, nothing coming out. My stomach felt like it was twisting and turning, hurting more than it'd ever had hurt before. My fingers dug into the seat until they turned white.

Michael pulled my hair out of my face, crouching behind me and rubbing my back.

"Oh God," I whispered, feeling something come up. "I think I ate or drank something bad last night."

My mind flickered to that party last night, and I cursed

myself. Maybe Linda had known we'd be there and told the cooks to fuck with me or something.

I wouldn't put it past her.

I pushed my head into the toilet and let it come up. All that wine from last night hurled into the toilet, sloshing back and forth in the water.

"That wine," I said, clutching my stomach. "Oh my God—"

He held my hair back tighter and stayed with me the entire time, rubbing my back as I puked my stomach out. Even when I finished, I felt like I needed to throw up more and more, but nothing would come out.

"You barely had any wine last night," Michael said. "Three sips at the most."

After sitting by the toilet for ten more minutes, I sat back and groaned. What the hell was that? Why'd I feel like I was about to puke up an entire—

"Let's get you in the shower," Michael said, turning on the shower until steam tumbled over the top of it.

I rested my head against the cupboard and moaned. The feeling of death was disappearing, so I hopped into the shower and hoped to God that it didn't happen again today.

After my shower and brushing my teeth a good three times to get rid of that nasty taste of wine, I found Michael in our bedroom, peering in his dresser. He closed it a bit too quickly and smiled at me.

"Still want to go out to breakfast?" he asked me. "Or we can stay home, and I can make us something if you're still feeling bad."

"Yes, I want to go. I'm feeling better. I think I needed to get it out of my system."

"Darrell's?"

A grin broke out on my face. "Darrell's."

\* \* \*

81

DARRELL'S WAS a tiny little breakfast shop, perched on a hillside, in Michael's neighborhood. It was pouring when we arrived, and by the looks of it, the place was busy. Michael grabbed the umbrella and opened my door for me, and together, we hurried to the entrance.

"Breakfast for two," Michael said.

The hostess led us into the one-room breakfast diner. With the entire back wall removed and replaced with sliding glass doors, we could see down the grassy hillside and all of the city from up here. The doors were cracked open, the sound of rain pattering against the ground outside filling my ears.

I sat in a seat across from Michael and gazed out the doors, smiling. "I already know what I want."

As if she'd overheard me, a waitress appeared at our table with a big smile and some water with lemon.

"Can I have pancakes with a side of oranges, please?"

The waitress turned toward Michael. "Number three," he said, handing her our menus. When she disappeared behind the counter, Michael raised a brow at me. "Oranges?"

"I've been craving them lately," I said, cheeks turning pink.

I grabbed his hands from across the table and sighed to myself. After last night, I felt so much better about us. We'd needed that talk, and we'd needed it bad. At least, I had.

For once in a long time, I didn't feel any awkwardness or anxiety being out with Michael. I wasn't ashamed of him by any means. He was smart, mature, good-looking, had his life together —everything I'd ever wanted in a man. But the stares were what got me.

I didn't know what it was, but I felt better than I had ever felt in my entire life.

I stared at him and kicked my legs back and forth, inter-locking our fingers.

"Not afraid to be seen with me today?" he asked.

"I'm never afraid to be seen with you," I said, touching my

fingers to his knuckles. "I just don't like the stares …" I scooted closer to him, still feeling those butterflies inside of me. "But *fuck them*."

"Fuck them?" Michael chuckled.

I curled my fingers around the collar of his shirt and pulled him toward me. "Fuck them. I want you."

I pressed my lips on his and kissed him long and hard, giving him all I had. Not caring if people were staring. Not caring that this might not look right to some people. Caring only about Michael, only about us.

When I pulled away, I rested my forehead against his. "I'm sorry for being so annoying and insecure lately. I don't want you to feel bad about this, because I really love you. I'm going to try to not let my insecurities get in the way."

After a few moments, Michael sipped on his water. "I accept your apology on one condition."

"And what's that?"

"You tell me when you fell in love with me," he said.

My heart felt all warm and fuzzy, a grin breaking out on my face. I hadn't gotten a chance to tell him last night. After we'd talked, I had fallen face-first into our mattress and into a deep sleep.

I squeezed his hands tighter. "I fell in love with you every time you showed up at the hospital. Every night you were there, you brought me dinner, and asked me how I was, and made me smile, and told me that you'd be there for me, no matter how difficult it got." I leaned across the table and trailed my thumb across his stubble. "It wasn't a moment. It was your support, your love, your heart … you."

# CHAPTER 21

MIA

"*M*ia," Dr. Xiao said after class on Monday.

I pushed my books into my backpack and smiled at her.

She waited for the last few students to leave the class and rubbed my shoulder. "How's everything going? Your mother?"

"I'm going to see her tonight with one of my friends. She's still struggling with making new memories, but at least she's alive and healthier now."

"And Michael?"

I thought back to this past weekend. Everything had seemed to have gone to complete shit, then gotten so much better. I nodded, a grin breaking out on my face. "I feel good," I said, the feelings so certain inside of me. "Michael and I talked, and … and it was so refreshing."

My chest tightened, my fingers tingling at the thought. "I'd needed to talk, and I'd needed it badly. I kept it bottled up for so long, thought that he wouldn't understand everything I was going through in silence … but he did."

"That's amazing, Mia," she said, eyes lighting up the entire lecture hall. She closed her laptop and placed it into her bag. "It's difficult to get out there and talk to someone about your worries. I'm so proud of you for having the courage to do that."

Upon hearing her words, I smiled even wider. "People are still spreading rumors, talking down about us … but I honestly think we can make it now. Before, I was unsure. The thought of breaking up with him crossed my mind, but I kept pushing." And it felt beyond weird to say it aloud, but I was damn proud of myself.

"Good, Mia. This is a great first step in healing. You've acknowledged your pain. You've talked it out with someone. It might be a bumpy ride, but you can do it. I believe you and Michael will become stronger from this."

I walked with her toward the door. "I sure hope so."

Because we were together for the long run.

* * *

After class, I picked Serena up at her house and drove us to St. Barbars. Serena had been asking to see Mom for a while now, and I knew she wanted to gush to her about something. Mom had always been there for her and Melissa when we were young. No matter what Dad had put her through, she always made sure that we were happy.

"Friends are most important. They'll be with you through everything," she always used to tell me.

Serena looped her arm around mine and walked into the assisted living center with me. Carol sat at the front desk and pushed the sign-in sheet to me without saying a word. She still looked embarrassed after I'd called her out the other day.

When we walked away, Serena stuck her name tag to her

chest. "What was that all about?" she asked, glancing back at Carol.

"Just someone who couldn't mind her business."

Serena's eyes widened. "Oh my gosh. Did you tell her off?" When I didn't answer, she squealed, earning her some hard stares from the nurses. "You did, didn't you?! Yes, girl, growing a backbone."

I playfully rolled my eyes and knocked on Mom's door.

"Come in," Mom called.

Serena and I walked into the room to see Mom clicking off the television.

"There is some raunchy stuff they play here," she said, fanning herself. "Oh God, give me a sec. Recovering from that boat scene still."

I let out a small laugh, knowing exactly what movie she must've been watching, and sat down on the bed next to her.

She pushed herself to a seated position. "How's everything, sweetheart? How'd the dinner go?"

"What dinner?"

"Michael's work dinner."

"You remembered I had a party to go to?"

She smiled widely at me. "Of course I did! Why would I forget about something like that? I told you things between you and him are getting pretty serious."

Warmth exploded through my chest. Mom had her memories back. She finally had her memories back, and I couldn't have ever been happier about anything. I wrapped my arms around her and pulled her into a tight hug.

She patted my back. "Mia, what's going on?"

I shook my head and slid into the bed with her, resting my head against her shoulder. "Nothing, Mom. I'm just glad you're back."

After letting out a confused laugh, she dropped it and turned to us. "So? Are you going to leave me hanging? How'd it go?" She glanced at Serena. "Has she told you yet?"

Serena placed a hand on her hip. "No, she's been waiting until we came to see you." She pulled up a chair. "So, spill."

My lips curled into a smile, and I shook my head. "It was okay. Drama with his coworkers that I don't want to get into."

"Thinking you're too young for him?" Serena asked, rolling her eyes. "Fuck them."

I laughed and shrugged. "Well, Michael and I talked about it, which was good, and … I learned I had an orange addiction this weekend, so that's a … plus?"

"Oranges?" Mom asked, brow raised. "A craving for them?"

"Yeah. Why?"

She blushed and waved it off as nothing. But it was something. I could see it on her face, in her eyes as they traveled to my stomach for a moment. I placed a hand over my stomach to cover my belly and sat up taller.

"So, *Eden* …" Serena said. She only called my mom by her first name when she wanted to spill something to her, and acted as if she were one of us, back in all the drama. "I got some *tea* for you." She smirked at me. "Your daughter is *ser-i-ous* about a certain Mr. Bryne."

Mom widened her eyes. "I knew it!" She leaned forward, her eyes glistening. "Tell me all about it." Mom looked at me. "I know Mia is holding back."

"Guess what he told her."

"What?"

"That he wanted to spend his life with her, Eden! *His life!*"

I rolled my eyes playfully, unable to hold back the biggest grin. My stomach felt like it had butterflies inside of it, fluttering around, making me feel all warm and fuzzy.

Mom and Serena started gossiping back and forth like they were old friends, and I knew it was good for both of them, so I shut up and let it happen. Plus, it made me feel all giddy inside, so I didn't mind that much.

As I lay there and listened, my phone buzzed in my pocket, and I pulled it out.

**Michael: I'll be home late.**

I frowned at the message because I wanted to jump for joy in his arms because Mom had gotten her memories back. Beyond excited. Over the moon. I couldn't even begin to explain how I was feeling at that moment. No matter the pain, heartbreak, hurt that I felt ... everything seemed to be coming back together.

# CHAPTER 22

MICHAEL

*A*fter filling out the rest of the paperwork for this damn restraining order, I submitted it at the courthouse and was told someone would get in touch about a court date to get it approved. I walked out of the courthouse and sat in my car. I was sure it wasn't often that a man filed for a restraining order against his ex-wife, but Linda had been taking things up a notch.

It had gone from texting me to showing up at my house to visiting Mia at work when she thought I wouldn't be there. What would she do next? Try to hurt Mia? I wasn't about to take any chances.

I pushed my phone into my pocket after sending Mia a text and started the car, heading onto the highway and passing the exit to our home.

I'd lied to Mia over text.

I didn't have to work late.

I needed to go see her mother.

After pulling into the St. Barbars' parking lot, I spotted Mia's car, parked on the other side of the building, and waited for her to come out so I could go see her mother. My stomach was in knots for the entire fifteen minutes.

Mia and Serena came out of the building, big smiles on their faces. My lips twisted into one, too, as I watched her, standing there in an off-white dress, the wind blowing it against her legs, moonlight bouncing off her face.

I couldn't believe I was going to actually do this. It was getting real. So damn real.

Once she got into her car with Serena, she texted me.

**Mia: Mom finally has her memories back! I'll see you at home.** <3

She backed out of the parking spot and drove off, tail lights disappearing into the night. My heart tightened at her message, beating faster and faster. I undid my seat belt and hurried into the assisted living center, knowing that visiting hours would be ending soon.

Carol greeted me at the front desk with a big, *forced* smile. "Coming to see your father?"

"Ms. Stevenson."

Her eyes widened, cheeks reddening, and then she nodded. "Of course."

She pushed the sign-in notebook to me, and I scribbled my name. When I finished, I gave her the notebook back and leaned across the counter.

"Do me a favor, Carol, and don't mention this to Mia when you see her."

Carol looked surprised, and then she nodded. "Okay," she said quietly.

She seemed off since the last time I had seen her. Maybe something had happened with Mia.

I brushed it off as nothing and walked through the halls until I reached Mia's mother's room. My chest felt tight, and I swallowed all my insecurities, knocking on the doorframe.

The door was open slightly, and her mother called out the door, "Mia, is that you again? Did you forget something?"

I peered my head into the room, and she smiled widely.

"Michael."

My heart raced, and I swore I could feel myself starting to sweat. I didn't know why I was getting so worked up about this. It wasn't the first time I had asked the question to a woman's parents. But last time ... it had been expected of me. I'd had a child to raise.

Now ... this was what I really wanted.

Mia was what I wanted.

This meant a lot to me.

Eden was the closest person to Mia. And I wanted to show Mia that I was more serious about this than I had been about anything in my entire life. She wasn't some fresh pussy to me. She wasn't someone I would ever give up on, no matter how hard it became between us.

She was mine, my Mia.

I wasn't going to leave when times got tough, when rumors about us were spreading like wildfire around the town because of my ex-wife. Nothing would stop me from loving Mia with all I had.

"Mia just left. You missed her," she said.

I stepped into the room. "I actually wanted to talk to you."

With wide eyes, she pushed herself to a sitting position, tilted her head, and grinned up. "About what?"

There was a lump in my throat, and for a moment, I felt like I couldn't breathe. This was real. I was really doing this. I swallowed it and took another step into the room. "About Mia."

She nodded to a chair next to her bed, and I took a deep breath, inhaling Mia's perfume. When I was about to come out with it, she placed a frail hand on my wrist and smiled.

"Mia loves you more than anything—I hope you know that. She's never really had a strong man in her life. She's afraid to love

—really, truly love—Michael. But I can see it in her eyes when she talks about you."

My heart warmed. I knew Mia loved me. It had taken everything I had to tell her about Linda and my past the other night. But when she'd looked over at me ... God, it was like ... I didn't even have words for it.

"I love her too." I smiled.

A smile tugged at her lips. "Good." She released my wrist. "Now, what do you want to talk about?"

I rubbed my sweaty palms together and tried to roll the tension out of my neck. But when I couldn't, I said *fuck it* and decided to come out with it already. "I want to spend the rest of my life with Mia, and I wanted to ask you if—"

"Are you asking what I think you're asking?" she asked me before I could continue, a sparkle in her wide eyes. She hadn't even let me finish. She gulped, tears filling her eyes. "Because yes. One hundred percent yes! Mia deserves someone like you in her life forever," she said, so much emotion on her face and in her voice.

# CHAPTER 23

MIA

"*M*ichael!" I shouted, jumping into his arms as soon as he walked through the door. I wrapped my arms around his shoulders and locked my legs around his waist, pulling him tightly to me. "Michael, my mom has her memories back!"

I could barely contain my excitement. I had been waiting for about an hour since I'd left St. Barbars for him to come home, so I could celebrate with him. Everything felt like it was coming together, like my life was finally back on track. In a few weeks, I'd have my degree. Mom was back. My relationship with Michael felt so much less stressful after our talk.

Nothing could stop me.

He wrapped his arms around my waist and buried his face into my neck, dropping his briefcase by the door. "That deserves a celebration," he said against my skin. Instead of walking up to the bedroom, he walked down the stairs to the sliding glass doors.

"The pool?" I asked.

Before I could even wiggle out of his hold, he threw me into the deep end of the pool. I sank under, my white dress getting wet, and swam to the top, breathing deeply as I emerged from the water.

"Michael!" I shouted playfully, blinking the water out of my eyes.

I pushed the wet hair out of my face and smiled up at Michael, who was shimmying out of all his clothes—suit, underwear, and all. He jumped in next to me, hands immediately finding my waist. Pushing me against the side of the pool, he kissed me and pulled my wet dress over my head.

"Mia," he teased me back, mumbling the word against my mouth. His cock was against my stomach, his fingers gliding up my sides.

Completely bare to him, I kicked my feet back and forth to hold myself up. He took my arms and placed them on the edge of the pool on the concrete and moved even closer to me, wrapping a hand around my chin and pulling my face toward his.

"Mia," he whispered again. "Hold your legs apart for me. Let me fuck you."

"In the pool?" I whispered, my nipples aching already.

He slipped a hand between my legs and rubbed my clit. "In the pool. On the patio. Everywhere."

And then he kissed me. He pushed the head of his cock inside of me, and I moaned loudly when he drove all of himself into me.

My hips moved back and forth against him, my tits bouncing around above the water. I threw my head back, feeling his hands glide around my waist as he drove me against the side of the pool and fucked me more roughly.

"Next time I fuck you in the pool," he mumbled against my ear, "we won't be the only ones here."

A raspy laugh escaped my lips, and I drew my fingers through his wet hair. "You're bad," I said, thinking back to all the times he had fucked me with people around. In his house, at the pool party, in the hospital.

We had been so close to getting caught, yet Michael loved it.

And part of me did too.

"You love it, Mia," he said into my ear, fingers moving faster against my clit. "It excites you more than anything, doesn't it?"

My pussy pulsed on his cock, the pressure building inside me. I sucked on my bottom lip and furrowed my brows at him.

With sparkling gray eyes, he looked up at me and smirked. "Doesn't it?" He dipped his head and sucked one of my nipples into his mouth, biting down gently. "Knowing that at any moment, someone could see these beautiful fucking tits bouncing as I thrust my cock into you?"

"Michael, I—" I grasped on to his shoulders, unable to suppress the rising force. "Michael, I'm going to—"

"Don't come yet, Mia," he said. "I'm not done with you."

He wrapped his arms around my waist and walked with me up the pool stairs. My legs were wrapped tightly around his waist, and his cock was still buried deep inside of me. He pounded into me over and over and over again and rested me against one of the pool chairs. Crawling up onto it with me, he continued to pound into me.

Ecstasy rolled through my body. I could feel every inch of him pumping in and out of me, filling me. Water dripped down his body and onto mine. I tangled my hands into his hair, tugging on it.

He kissed down my body, sucking on my neck and definitely leaving little red marks on it. Then, he kissed down my breasts, tugging my nipple into his mouth and tugging on it roughly. I arched my back and let out a loud moan, the sensation driving me wild.

"Harder, Michael," I moaned, nails digging into his back. "Please."

I gripped the edge of the pool chair until my knuckles turned white. He hooked one arm under my thigh, spreading my legs and ramming himself deeper and deeper inside of me. Tension rose in my core, and I curled my toes.

Oh my God ... how could one man feel so fucking good? My pussy was clenching so much that I felt like I was about to—

"Come for me, Mia." Michael buried his face into the crook of my neck. "I want to hear you scream my name."

The pressure was almost too much to bear. I scurried away from him and up the pool chair, taking his cock out of me and squirming around to try to ease the pain between my legs.

But Michael followed me up the pool chair, hooked his arm around my thigh again, and pulled me back down to him. "Don't run from me."

He plunged himself back inside of me, and I screamed out his name, the pleasure unbearable.

"Michael!" I whimpered, nails digging into his back. "Michael, my God. Michael."

Wave after wave washed over me. Tingles ran up and down my thighs. Michael sucked lightly on my neck, his stubble tickling me.

"Come inside of me," I breathed into his ear so desperately. My mind was in a daze. "Please come inside of me."

Michael groaned against me and slowed down his pace, his cum dripping out of my pussy. When he pulled out, he lay on top of me for a few moments, lightly kissing my neck. After giving me a long kiss on the mouth, he grabbed a blanket from inside and pulled it over our shoulders, starting a fire in the firepit. I rested my head against his shoulder, letting the pool water drip down my legs.

"What're you thinking about?" I asked, staring at the flames.

"This Friday," he said, "I'm taking you and your friends out."

"Me and all my friends?" I asked, brow raised at him.

"It could just be us, but I think you'll want them there."

Butterflies fluttered in my stomach, and I smiled. "What're we going to do?"

"Dinner and ... a surprise."

# CHAPTER 24

MIA

$\mathcal{I}$t was Wednesday afternoon, and I was downtown at Dunkin' again—my new favorite spot to study—with two orange peels sitting on the table next to me and a large iced coffee. My mind was wandering from my psych homework to this Friday, when Michael had said he was going to take me out with Serena, Damien, and Victor.

I believed Michael was going to ask Melissa to come, but I wasn't sure she'd show up. She hadn't talked to me or even reached out in over a few weeks now. I wasn't sure Michael had talked any sense into her either.

My phone buzzed on the table, and I flipped it over.

**Mason: I love you more than anything.**

**Mason: Please answer me.**

**Mason: I'd do anything to get you to love me again, to hold you.**

My eyes widened at the last message, something not sitting

right with me. I took a deep breath, screenshotted everything he had sent me over the past twenty-four hours, and sent it to Serena. It had gotten much worse today for some reason. I didn't know why, but there seemed to be a certain type of urgency from him now.

And it made me feel uncomfortable.

Instead of not telling Michael like I'd first wanted to, I sent him a message at work with the screenshots attached. I trusted Michael, and I wanted him to trust me. Something about the way he'd reacted last time I told him about Mason made me want to never hide anything like that from him again.

If I wanted to heal and to spend my life with Michael, I needed to believe in him as much as he believed in me. No more hiding what was happening. No more keeping it to myself. I needed to confront the truth and stop being so whiny about it.

Michael responded almost instantly.

**Michael: Send these to Melissa and then block Mason. I know you're doing this for her, but she's seen multiple messages from him to you. And she has done nothing about it. I'll try to talk to her again when I get off work. But I don't want you getting hurt.**

**Michael: Please block his number and cut off contact.**

**Michael: For me.**

I gulped and nodded to myself. Michael was right. Melissa had seen his messages. Serena must've sent her the screenshots. I was sure of it because the next day, she had come to visit Michael, yet she hadn't broken it off with Mason.

It hurt to know that she refused to see how bad Mason was for her. I wanted to believe that he treated her differently, that *that* was the reason she hadn't broken up with him … but coming to see me, sending me these messages showed me that he was the same old Mason. Refusing to take responsibility for his actions. Cheating on Melissa. Being a damn prick.

For the first time in a long time, I tapped on Melissa's name in my messages and attached the screenshots without any message. My finger hovered over the Send button, my heart pounding against my chest.

*Please, Melissa, believe me. Get out of this relationship for your own sake.*

After I gathered all my courage, I hit the Send button, praying that she'd read them, that she hadn't blocked me, that she'd realize something wasn't right.

I waited a few moments and watched the Delivered message turn into Read. Three little bubbles popped up on the screen, signaling that she was responding to me. But they disappeared almost as quickly as they'd appeared.

Five minutes passed. Then ten.

The bubbles appeared again—this time for longer—then they disappeared completely.

My heart sank in my chest. Sure, our friendship was on the rocks right now, but I wanted what was best for her. And it wasn't Mason … I was sure of that.

Another message from Mason popped up on the phone.

**Mason: I'll do anything to get you back, Mia. Anything at all. You'll see.**

There was an undertone to his message that gave me the chills. After scrunching my nose, I tapped onto the message. There were three tiny bubbles, showing me that he was typing still. Why couldn't he get the damn hint and leave me alone? I hadn't responded to any of his messages.

I navigated to his contact information, deciding not to wait for his message to come through before I hit the block button and locked him out of my life for good. All his messages disappeared, and I didn't have to deal with his ass anymore unless he started to show up at Serena's house again.

I was done with him for good.

At least, that was what I told myself.

But in the pit of my stomach, I knew that wouldn't be the last time I heard from Mason.

He'd be back.

# CHAPTER 25

MICHAEL

*M*e: Meet me at Rattlesnake's Bar. 5 p.m. We need to talk.

I stared down at the phone on the bar, tapping my foot against the ground and waiting for Melissa to show. She'd read the message three hours ago and not responded. I wondered if she'd even show up tonight.

The bartender leaned over the counter toward me and handed me my second drink. "Drinking alone tonight, babe?"

After sliding the phone into my pocket, I grimaced at her. "Waiting for someone."

She raised her brows and nodded toward the other side of the bar. "Wouldn't be that pretty lady, would it?" There was a woman sitting at the other side, her blonde hair cascading down her shoulders in curls, brown eyes fixed on me. The bartender slid me a piece of paper. "She wanted me to give you this."

I glanced down at the woman's number and pushed it back across the bar toward her. "I'm taken," I said.

"I don't see any ring on your finger," she said.

My lips pressed together. Damn, did nobody respect relationships these days? I took a deep breath and tried to think clearly because when Melissa walked through the door, I needed to try to talk some sense into her. It'd be hopeless if I started the conversation angry.

"There's about to be." I turned back to my phone and sipped on my whiskey, letting it burn the back of my throat.

The bartender disappeared and struck up a conversation with the woman who looked to be her friend. I took another deep breath.

*Come on, Melissa. Where are you?*

The door opened, and Melissa walked into the room. Bags under her eyes. Hair in knots. Makeup drawn on in an attempt to look like she had everything put together.

When she saw me, she gave me a half-smile and slid onto the seat next to mine. "Hey."

I looked her up and down. She looked so tired and broken. I hated not being able to do anything about it. I wanted her back, needed to make sure she was safe. Yet I couldn't make her choices for her.

"Hey," I said, lifting my hand to a different bartender. "Can she get a—"

"A water," Melissa said. "A water is fine."

I nodded. "Just a water."

After the bartender filled a glass for her, I turned toward Melissa and frowned. God, what had I done wrong? Why wouldn't she leave him already? Couldn't she see how shitty he was? I mean, she had to feel different.

"How are you and Mia?" Melissa asked.

"That's not what I wanted to talk about."

"But I want to know." She took a sip of her water and looked up at me.

I wasn't sure if she was trying to push back the conversation or if she really, truly wanted to know.

She seized my wrist. "I really do."

A grin broke out on my face, one that I tried to suppress almost immediately. But no matter how much I tried, I couldn't.

Melissa gave me a trying smile. "I'm sorry for being such a bitch to you guys. It seems like she makes you so happy."

"I know it's difficult for you," I said. "But I love her. A lot. And I won't stop loving her. I want to spend the rest of my life with her."

She held my wrist tighter. "I know," she said quietly. "And I'm okay with that."

My eyes widened. "You are?"

"Yes …" Her voice was quiet. "It took me a while to understand, but I've realized my mistakes, and I want to apologize for how shitty I've been lately. I have a lot going on and am under a lot of stress right now."

Part of me wanted to jump for joy. Melissa was coming around. Very slowly. But she was learning that life wasn't all frat boys and parties. It was hard work, stress, decisions, and consequences.

But I still wanted to see her succeed and be happy. After dealing with all her mother's shit, she deserved it.

"We're going out on Friday night. You should join us."

Melissa frowned. "I would, but I have to work."

Suddenly, she got quiet and sipped her water, rubbed a hand across her face to wipe away any sort of stress, and sighed. "What'd you want to talk about?"

We were in such a good place that I didn't want to ruin it by bringing Mason up. She'd just get angry with me again. But I couldn't handle it anymore.

"Did you get the messages from Mia today?" I asked, fingers gripping my glass.

She looked down at the water and took a sip. "Yeah, I did."

I pursed my lips, waiting for her to continue but she didn't. "And?"

"And nothing."

"Nothing?" I asked. "What do you mean, nothing?"

A look of fear crossed her face, and I ached to pull her to my chest like I had when she was a girl and afraid of scary movies.

She shook her head. "Nothing is going to happen."

"You're not breaking up with him?"

"No." That single word was filled with such sorrow. "I can't."

Anger and rage burned inside of me. "He doesn't love you, Melissa. If he's doing that with Mia, who knows how many other girls he's been with? You need to understand that—"

She slammed her hand against the bar, making me stop mid-sentence. "You need to understand that the situation is more complicated than you think it is. I can't just leave him." Her voice fell with every word, and all I could feel was fear.

This wasn't Melissa. Something was keeping her there, and I didn't know if it was Mason or something more.

"Dad, I have something to tell you," she said, fear laced in every one of her words. "Please don't get mad at me."

There wasn't much more I could get angry at Melissa for. We had both done so much these past few months. I wanted to forgive her. Get her better, sleeping, healthy again. She looked so tired and sick.

"What is it, Melissa?" I asked. "I won't get angry with you."

"Promise me?"

"I promise you."

She took a deep breath, gulped, and then said the one thing I'd never expected from her in a million fucking years. "Dad, I'm pregnant."

# CHAPTER 26

MICHAEL

*E*verything seemed to freeze. I thought I'd misheard her. Melissa couldn't be pregnant, especially not with that asshole's kid. She might've been adventurous, but she had always been safe. I couldn't believe what I had heard.

"You're pregnant?" I asked, my voice barely a whisper. I looked up at her face. "Melissa ... pregnant?"

She gnawed on the inside of her lips. "I'm sorry," she whispered.

I parted my lips and pressed them back together. All I could think about was how I had been in her position twenty-two years ago. I'd felt so alone, especially after my father kicked me out and told me to figure shit out for myself. I couldn't let the same thing happen to Melissa.

"No, I'm sorry for kicking you out."

"You're not angry?"

"No, I'm not angry," I said quietly. Yet I felt a pain in my heart because I had hurt Melissa by throwing her out. Maybe if I'd spent more time with her or paid more attention to her, she would've been safer when with Mason.

She gulped, and I knew there was more to the story.

I grabbed her shoulder and squeezed lightly. "What is it, Melissa?"

Sadness and anguish washed over her face, and she frowned deeply. She shook her head, as if she didn't want to talk about it, yet I could see the tears building in her eyes. I knew she wasn't about to tell me. I knew that begging for her to come home was hopeless.

"If you're not going to tell me, please come home," I begged.

"I can't."

"I can help you with the pregnancy, Melissa. You need to be eating healthy, getting sleep, and making changes to your life. You can't do that with Mason. I know guys like him. He's probably out at parties every weekend, telling you to come with him, throwing himself and his future away."

She pushed her shoulders back and wiped a tear from her cheek with her thumb.

When she didn't say anything, my eyes widened. "He doesn't know, does he?"

"I'm going to tell him tonight."

I rubbed my forehead and swore under my breath. "Are you sure it's his and not Victor's?"

"Yes, I know. I just... I know it's not his," she whispered, sipping her water and acting as if this were normal and that everything was okay, but it wasn't.

She didn't know what she was getting into. She didn't know what kind of life she had ahead of her.

I did.

I had been through that with her mother.

But I was conflicted on what to say next. I didn't know if Mason would settle down and take up his responsibilities. Sometimes, having a kid changed people for the better; other times ...

it didn't change them at all. He could mature like I had, or he could stay the same old Mason. And part of me, deep down, knew that he'd stay the same old Mason. He wouldn't change. He was still texting Mia, for God's sake. If he really loved Melissa as much as she'd told me he did, he would've stopped trying to contact his ex-girlfriend.

"You have to leave him. Come back home. We'll help you take care of your baby," I said, speaking for Mia and me.

Mia might've had a rockier relationship with Melissa than I did, but she cared about her. And I knew Mia wouldn't let her stay in that relationship with a baby.

It wasn't only that I wanted Melissa to be healthy during the pregnancy either. I wanted her to be happy and healthy after it too. Her mother had had postpartum depression for the entire year after Melissa was born. I'd watched her go through hell and back every single day with mood swings, panic attacks, fatigue, and intrusive thoughts. A lump formed in my throat. I'd tried to get her the best care we could afford, but it wasn't enough back then. I'd thought I was going to lose her, and I didn't want Melissa to feel that way.

I knew I couldn't stop those feelings after the pregnancy, if it did happen. But I could be there with her. I could help her through it. Just like her mother had needed a supportive partner and friends, Melissa would need that too.

Added stress would harm her.

Melissa shook her head again. "I can't. I want Mason to be part of the baby's life."

"It'll be a toxic environment for that baby," I said. "It was toxic when you were growing up, and I wish I'd gotten divorced from your mother long before I actually had the courage and strength to do it."

"I didn't come here to have you talk to me about leaving him," she said, putting her foot down. "I just wanted to let you know."

"But, Melissa—"

"Dad, please. I want him in his baby's life. I'm not going to take that away from him."

I balled my hands into fists. I hated Mason, more than I'd ever thought I would, but it was Melissa's life I had to think about.

She tilted her head down and glanced at the table. "What if Mom had taken me away from you? What if she never even told you she was pregnant with me?" she asked, brows furrowed together. "You would have no idea I even existed. You wouldn't be my dad, just a stranger." There was a spark in her eyes, and she leaned forward, trying to hit the point right where it hurt. "Mom told me that before you found out she was pregnant, you were just like Mason. Partied. Drank. Did shit that you wouldn't dare do now."

I pursed my lips, trying not to get angry. "I was nothing like him. I didn't cheat. I didn't treat your mother like shit. I respected her. I treated her well. I made sure she was happy even if I wasn't."

My chest tightened. I felt so ... so torn. But Melissa wouldn't change her mind until something happened, and I was afraid something bad would have to happen before she could think clearly about this.

She gulped and stood up. "I love and miss you, but I have to go."

Before she could leave, I grabbed her wrist. "Melissa, if you need anything, please come by the house. I don't want you feeling like I'm not here for you. I love you more than anything."

# CHAPTER 27

MIA

$\mathscr{I}$ walked out of the bathroom with a little black dress hugging my body and my makeup done to perfection for once. It was already Friday night, and I couldn't wait for one night of fun with my friends. I had been waiting all damn week for tonight.

Michael stood by his dresser and pushed something into his pocket just as I walked out. He looked me up and down, eyes widening. He grabbed me by the waist and pulled me toward him, nose in my hair, breathing me in. "You look so sexy," he said against my ear, yet there was something in his voice that sounded so taut.

I had heard it all week—something strained, something stressful. I moved my hand down his abdomen to the front of his pants, stroking him gently until he was hard.

"You're tense, Michael," I mumbled against his lips. "Let me help you out."

Dropping down to my knees in front of him, I let my fingers

run to his belt. We should have left by now if we wanted to get to the restaurant before everyone else did, but I wanted to please him. He had done so much for me these past few weeks that he deserved this and more.

He lightly grasped my chin and forced me to look up at him as I undid his button and pulled down his zipper enough to see his bulge through his briefs. I ran my fingers over it and looked up at him, watching his body relax.

After pushing the spaghetti straps of my dress down my shoulders and letting my breasts slide out of it, I placed my mouth on the head of his cock through his underwear. I glanced up at him through my lashes, my pussy clenching.

My fingers curled around the waistband of his briefs, and I pulled it down inch by inch until the head of his cock appeared. I slowly started to suck each inch of him into my mouth, feeling the wetness beginning to pool between my legs.

When I pushed his underwear down enough and I sucked as much of him as I could into my mouth, I rested my hand around his balls and the base of his cock and began to bob my head back and forth on him. He let out a low sigh—one that I knew he had been holding for quite some time now—and caressed my jaw with his thumb.

"Mia," he groaned.

My clit ached, and I squeezed my thighs together, rubbing them back and forth to try to create any kind of friction between them. Faster, I bobbed my head on his cock, letting spit and drool start to run down my chin. All my makeup would be ruined tonight before we ever even left for dinner, yet I didn't care. I wanted this. I *needed* this.

Slipping my hand around the base of his cock, I pulled it out of my mouth, ducked my head under it, and lightly sucked his balls into my mouth. I continued to stroke him faster and faster as I stared up at him. He ran a hand through my hair.

"I want you to come all over my face, Michael. Rub your cum

in. Make me your dirty little slut for tonight." I stroked him faster, my hand tightening around his cock. "I want you to ruin me."

He tilted his head back and groaned, tightening his grip in my hair.

I sucked him back into my mouth until my lips met the base of his hips. And even then, I tried to get him further down my throat, tried to ease the pressure between my legs, tried to please him.

After grabbing his hand, I placed it on my neck, so he could feel how big he felt in my throat.

"Make me your slut," I tried to say with him still inside of me, but it came out so garbled and gaggy.

Spit rolled down my chin and onto my tits, making them glisten. Even though I couldn't take any more of him, I bobbed my head a few inches back and forth, trying to get more of him inside of me. God, I needed it more than anything. I loved pleasing him. I loved making him feel so damn good.

He groaned and tugged lightly on my hair, hand tightening around my throat. "My dirty little slut for tonight?" he asked, reluctant to say it because he was always so … so proper.

I knew he didn't like calling me a slut, I knew that I was so much more to him than that, but it felt so good and so dirty to hear him say it.

I slipped a hand between my legs and started to tease my clit, the tension rising. I nodded and stared up at him through teary eyes.

"I don't want to cover your face with my cum," he said. "I want you to feel it rolling down the back of your pretty little throat."

He pulled himself all the way out of me and crouched down to meet me eye to eye. "Can you do that for me?" he asked, gray eyes staring intensely into mine.

"Yes, Michael," I whispered.

He rubbed his thumb over the spit on my chin, and I grabbed

his hand, making him rub it all over my face. When I'd said I wanted him to ruin me, I'd wanted to be covered in spit and drool, swallowing his cum, sucking him off until he couldn't handle it any longer.

A dirty slut for tonight.

I rubbed small, quick circles around my swollen clit and moaned as he pushed the head of his cock against my lips.

"Please," I begged. "Give it to—"

He pushed himself inside of me until my lips met the base of his stiff cock and then began to face-fuck me. Sloppy, wet gagging sounds drifted from my throat. More spit and drool ran down my chin. I rubbed my pussy faster than I ever had as he fucked my throat.

My cheeks flushed, my eyes becoming watery. I ran my fingers up his thigh and curled them into his pants pocket to balance myself as his thrusts quickened. He tensed and pulled my hand away from it.

"Put your hands behind your back for me," he said, stilling in my throat. "I want to see your perky, big tits bounce."

I gagged on his cock and put one hand behind my back, still rubbing my pussy with the other. He glanced down at my body, gaze drifting from my tits to the hand between my legs.

"I bet that pussy is dripping, aching for a release, isn't it?"

When I didn't answer him, he gripped my hair tighter. "*Tell me* how good it feels, Mia."

I opened my mouth to say something else but could only gag on him.

"That good, huh?"

My pussy tightened, and I moaned on his cock. The force rose in my core, pushing me higher and higher and higher until I was about to tip over the edge. He gripped my chin and made me look up at him as he continued to pound into my mouth.

"You're going to come when I do," he said, running his fingers down my neck. "As soon as you feel my cum run down your throat, I want you to come so hard that you can't sit up straight."

I tightened even more, trying to hold myself back for that long. I didn't think I could. I was about to … about to …

He stilled inside of me, cum hitting the back of my throat, and my legs trembled harder than they ever had.

Rapture exploded through me, yet I didn't stop rubbing my pussy. I doubled over slightly, unable to hold myself up, but Michael tightened his grip around my throat and held me in place.

I whimpered and swallowed all his cum, the pleasure still pumping out of me. He pulled out, and I wanted nothing more than to curl into a ball and finish out my orgasm because this was the most intense thing I had ever experienced.

He crouched by my side, placed his hand above mine, and let it glide over my clit. I leaned into him, grasping on to his shoulders for support.

"Michael," I whispered, squeezing my eyes shut. "Michael, it feels so good."

When I finished, he pulled his hand away, scooped me into his arms, and set me on the bathroom toilet. After wetting a washcloth, he knelt by my side and washed all the spit, drool, and makeup off my face. His lips were set into a smile, yet there was still a tenseness in them.

"You ruined my makeup," I said, a grin breaking out on my face.

He wiped the last of it away, set the cloth in the sink, and placed a kiss on my lips. "You look better without it."

# CHAPTER 28

MIA

*A*fter I cleaned up in the bathroom, Michael glanced at himself in the mirror, still looking stiff. I stood behind him.

"Is something wrong?" I asked. I rubbed his back, rested my head on his shoulder, and stared at him through the mirror.

Ever since he had come home from his talk with Melissa the other day, he'd seemed off. I had asked that night if something happened, but he didn't really want to talk. But something had been bothering him.

"You've been tense and distant all week."

He stuffed his hand into his pocket, gave me a smile, then let it falter. "I … I've been …" He paused for a long time and grimaced. "There's something I need to tell you before we go out tonight. I wanted to tell you sooner, but I needed to think things through first."

My chest tightened, a lump forming in my throat. "What is it?"

Something didn't feel right, and I hoped that whatever it was, it wasn't about to interfere with our relationship. I didn't know if I could deal with any more drama at the moment. My heart had been flung around so much these past few months, and I wanted some peace.

"It's okay," I whispered, heart pounding in my chest. "You can tell me."

He turned to face me and gripped my fingers in his hands. "It's about Melissa."

"What about her?" I asked, brushing my thumbs against his knuckles. "Did something happen? Did Mason do something to her?" I clenched my jaw, thinking the absolute worst.

After I'd blocked Mason's number, I had known he'd do something, flip out most likely. He always thought he had me wrapped around his finger, thought I'd be that stupid girl for him forever. When he'd lost me, he'd lost his control and his power.

I grabbed his hand tighter. "Please don't tell me he …" I whispered, tears threatening to well in my eyes. Because I would criticize myself for it. He had a god-awful way of blaming other people for his mistakes, for taking his anger out on the one person he was supposed to love.

Mason had never hit me, never laid a hand on me like that … but he had done other things. Things that disturbed me down to my very core. Things that I stored deep into my memories and swore I would never reopen because if I did … I'd break down in tears for how weak I had been to let a man touch me when I never wanted to be touched.

Cue everything I slept with Mason for the past year.

Michael shook his head. "Melissa is pregnant."

My eyes widened. "Melissa is pregnant?" The words came out just as broken as his words had. Yet I couldn't believe it.

So many questions were running through my mind, and I couldn't stop them if I tried. *Is the baby Mason's or Victor's? Maybe she has slept with someone else? How far along is she? Has she told*

*Mason?* I sucked in a deep breath. No, she definitely hadn't yet. *How is she feeling without friends to help her through this time in her life?* She must feel so alone with nobody. Nobody, except Mason, who—let's face it—didn't love her at all.

I wrapped my arms around myself. I couldn't imagine being pregnant right now. Melissa was so young, still had so much of her life ahead of her.

"She needs to come back," I said to Michael, staring up into his eyes. "She can't stay with Mason during this. He's going to stress her out with going out, drinking, pressuring her into doing things she doesn't want to do …" The list went on and on.

Mason wouldn't physically hurt her, but who knew what'd happen when she started to gain weight, when she got *pregnant* pregnant? He'd comment on her weight. He'd cheat. He'd make her feel like complete shit.

Michael sighed deeply through his nose and rubbed his face. "I tried, Mia. I really did. I don't know what else to do. I asked her to come back, told her we'd help her out with everything. She doesn't want to listen to me. She's going to be falling into the same hole that I fell into."

"Michael," I whispered, grasping his face in my hands. "I know this sucks. I know that I won't ever know how you feel, but I'm going to do everything I can to try to get her back. She can't be there with him during her pregnancy." Unless he suddenly changed, but that wasn't going to happen.

Michael laid a hand over mine and gently rubbed it. "We can talk about this later. I want you to have a good time tonight. You deserve it."

I shook my head up at him. "But, Michael, we need to—"

"Mia, please," Michael said, pressing his lips on my forehead. "I want this night to be special. I don't want this to ruin it. I needed to tell you because it's been bothering me."

After relaxing under his touch, I tried to push away the thoughts of Melissa being with Mason. But as hard as I tried, I couldn't. Maybe I was stupid for feeling bad for Melissa and wanting to help her, but … it was what I would want her to do if she were in my position.

I couldn't let her go through this alone. I would fight for her even though she wouldn't do the same for me. I would tell Serena to visit her even if she didn't want to see me. I would make sure she and her baby had the best life even if she still refused to leave Mason after those text messages.

"Okay?" Michael whispered against my forehead, his body still tense.

"Okay," I said, guiding him toward the bedroom door. "Now, let me finish getting ready." I pushed him out of the room, closed the door, and took a deep breath.

After I grabbed my phone from the dresser, I found my text chat with Melissa.

**Me: If you don't want to talk about Mason, we don't have to talk about Mason. Just let me know that you're okay and tell me if there is anything I can ever do for you. I'm sorry about everything that's happened between us. I don't hate you for any of it. I care about you and want you to be safe and healthy.**

Though I didn't think she'd respond to me—because she hadn't the other day when I sent her those screenshots of Mason's chat—three little bubbles appeared under her name. I waited, and I waited, and I waited, my heart racing.

And then, after what seemed like years, she finally messaged me back.

**Melissa: I'm okay.**

My stomach dropped, and I felt so disappointed at the two-worded message. But something was better than—

**Melissa: I can't come tonight. I wish I could be there for you.**

I clutched my phone to my chest and smiled. Progress. This was progress.

# CHAPTER 29

MIA

*T*hough Michael had told me not to worry, Melissa was still on my mind throughout the night. I drowned myself in glass of water after glass of water at dinner, talking to Serena and trying to see if she knew about it yet. I'd tell her eventually, but not tonight since Michael wanted some peace and quiet.

And the drama that would unfold when Victor found out was beyond anything I wanted to deal with right now. Victor was already heartbroken because of Melissa. I didn't know what would happen when he learned she was pregnant now. With Mason's kid. *Is it Mason's?*

I leaned my head against Michael's shoulder. He wasn't as talkative as he had been the other night at his work party, probably because we were so much younger than him and he had no idea about the latest video games that Victor and Damien couldn't stop talking about.

But whatever it was that they were talking about didn't

bother me. Tonight was calm, peaceful even. I wished every night could be this relaxing.

I smiled at the guys and hooked my arm around Michael's, leaning in close to him.

Serena looked at me with her brows furrowed together. "So, have either of you heard from Melissa?"

I sat up. "I texted her the other day about Mason," I said, not sure if Michael wanted me to tell her about their meetup. My lips turned into a frown. "She didn't respond then, but she texted me before we left to come here and said that she was sorry she couldn't make it."

Serena looked surprised. "Really?"

Michael sat back and arched a brow. "She did?"

I nodded and looked at Serena. "Yes, she did."

While I had originally thought Victor was a sleazeball like Mason, my opinion of him had changed these past few months. Victor was actually a really amazing guy. He truly cared about the people he let in, and so he was taking this worse than I had taken it when I found out.

So, I leaned forward and lowered my voice, so the guys wouldn't hear us. When I was sure he and Damien weren't listening, I glanced back at Serena. "I think you should reach out to her again. See if there's anything she needs help with," I said, trying to convince Serena to go without giving away too much information about Melissa being pregnant.

Michael gripped my knee and squeezed. This was hard for him. All he wanted was for her to come back and stay with us, so he knew she was healthy during this. Yet she wouldn't. Maybe she thought Mason would change. Maybe she thought that him getting her pregnant would make him the kind of man that Michael was.

But I knew that a baby wasn't going to fix anything.

Mason would continue to damage her. Mason would continue to hurt her.

It didn't matter if she had his baby inside of her. He didn't care about her that much.

Serena frowned. "Every time I message her about Mason, she always shoots me down." She shook her head. "I don't know what to do. I've been trying for so long, but she doesn't want to hear it."

I reached across the table, grasped her hand in mine, and squeezed. "Please," I whispered. "Reach out to her once more. Ask her if she needs anything. Ask her how she's doing." I shrugged my shoulders, not knowing what else to say.

Serena furrowed her brows. "Is something wrong with her?"

"No," I said too quickly.

She gave me that *yeah, right* look, but I shook my head and shot her a *I can't say anything about it* look back because I couldn't. It wasn't my place, especially when Michael was in the position he was in.

When the guys turned back to us, Serena dropped it, and Michael leaned closer to me.

"Thank you," he whispered into my ear.

Victor smiled at me. "So, Mia, I heard your mom is getting better."

My heart warmed, and I nodded. Everything was coming together. Slowly. My life was finally taking a positive turn, and I felt like I was actually getting somewhere. When I had been with Mason, I'd felt like I was running around in circles, not ever getting anywhere, trying to keep my head above water.

But now, nothing could stop me.

Not a deadbeat dad. Not a crazy ex-wife. Not even an ex-boyfriend.

After finishing the last of my burger, I pushed my plate toward the center of the table and rested a hand on my stomach. I could eat more, but I wanted dessert. When I had looked through the dinner menu, I had seen they had orange bars. And you bet I was saving room for that.

"Are you hungry for dessert?" Michael asked, nose grazing against my ear.

I pushed my thighs together, suddenly hit with a need to pee my bladder out. "Let me go to the restroom before we order." I stood up, surveying the crowded restaurant for the restroom. All the way across the room, near the bar, there was an entrance to the restroom.

After pressing my lips on his, I pushed through the crowd to get to the restroom. So much water. Why'd I drink so much? I hurried to the room, wanting to get in and out of there quickly because I was having such a good time with Michael and my friends. It was the first time in a long time that I'd felt so damn good about us. I didn't want the night to end.

Michael called my name. At least, I thought it was Michael. But I didn't turn back because I was about one second from pissing myself in front of everyone. My hands glided against the cold wooden restroom door, and I pushed it open.

One moment, I was walking toward the restroom stall to pee, and the next moment, someone had their hands on my hips, gripping me quite harshly. At first, I thought Michael had followed me into the restroom to finish what we'd started earlier. But when I was pushed against the sink counter and I could finally look into the mirror, I screamed.

It wasn't Michael. It wasn't Serena. It was Mason.

# CHAPTER 30

MIA

*B*efore I could scream again, he snaked his hand around the front of my throat and squeezed. He pressed his cock against my ass and placed his lips to my ear. "Shh, shh, shh."

I let out another gargled yell and threw my heel back into his shin. "Get off of me!" I shouted, struggling as pee literally ran down my thigh because I couldn't hold it in any longer. "You're fucking crazy!"

I pushed and squirmed in his grasp, but he was stronger than I was.

*Has he fucking followed me to this restaurant? Is he stalking me or some crazy shit?*

"Stop, Mia. I just want to talk," he said against me, words slurred.

"Stop, Mason!" I threw back my elbow and hit him in the ribs. "Get off of me."

Yet he didn't budge.

Trying as much as I could, I turned myself around in his hold, so I was facing him. He grinded his entire body into me, his chest against my chest, his breath in my ear, his hardness against my stomach. All I could smell was so much alcohol on his breath.

"You're mine, Mi—"

I kneed him right in the balls. One time. Two times. Three times. Until he stumbled back in pain, clutching his testicles. I sprinted past him and out of the restroom as quickly as I could. Tears welled up in my eyes. My hands were shaking. I couldn't think straight.

*Oh my God.*

*Oh my God.*

I needed to get away. I needed to leave here. I couldn't let him touch me like that again.

There were so many damn people here. I tried to squeeze between them all. I glanced back to see Mason coming out of the restroom, gaze locked on me and only me. My heart pounded against my chest.

*Michael. Where is Michael?*

I needed Michael.

Yet I couldn't seem to see straight.

Someone snatched my wrist and pulled me back toward them. I let out another scream as Mason roughly wrapped his arm around me from behind. I threw my elbow back, hitting him in the ribs again, and turned around, about to scream at him to get away from me, when Michael grabbed him by the shoulder and hurled him backward.

Mason stumbled into a bunch of people at the bar, and Michael went at him harder than Victor had a few weeks ago. Punch after punch after punch, Michael landed them on Mason's pretty-boy face. Blood spewed out of Mason's nose, and his eyes turned black and blue almost instantly.

Serena grabbed my shoulders, holding me back. "Oh my gosh, are you okay?"

Tears streamed down my face, and I tried to get out of her

hold … but my entire body was trembling in fear. Mason landed a solid punch right on Michael's face, and I screamed for him. I felt so fucking helpless. I needed to do something.

I squirmed away from Serena, but another set of hands clamped down on my shoulders. Victor held me back, hands tight on my body, jaw clenched. Drinks were spilling everywhere. Glass was breaking. Couples were hurrying away from the fight.

"She's mine," Mason shouted at Michael in the midst of the fight.

Someone tried to pull Michael off Mason, but Michael wouldn't budge. He continued to kick the shit out of Mason until Mason's head rolled back and he collapsed against the bar, unable to even stand on his own. And even then, Michael held him up by the collar and rained punches down on him.

There was so much pain and anger in every punch, every kick.

Blue and red flashing lights appeared by the window, and I gulped. The cops. The cops were here. I needed to get Michael away from Mason before something worse happened. Yet I couldn't move. I felt so violated. I felt so weak. I felt so … so good, watching Michael hurt Mason for everything that he had done.

Michael had never been a violent man, but to see how strong, how protective, how possessive he was over me … it made me love him even more in some fucked up way. Michael wasn't a boy like Mason was. Michael was a man. A good, kind man who'd do anything to protect the people he loved.

# CHAPTER 31

MICHAEL

*A*ll this pent-up anger seemed to flow right out of me as I beat on Mason until he couldn't stand straight. For every text he'd sent Mia. For every time he'd hurt Mia. For getting Melissa pregnant, then showing up here without a care in the fucking world. It all came out, and I couldn't stop it.

"Michael, stop, please …" Mia said, voice full of panic and heartbreak.

I tried to gather myself, knowing that I'd let my emotions get the best of me, and stepped back. But Mason threw another punch and landed it on my jaw. Mia let out another scream, but Victor held her back.

"The cops, Michael. The cops are here."

Suddenly, someone grabbed me by the shoulder and yanked me back, pressing me against the wall. I cursed under my breath, feeling my eyes starting to swell, and refused to meet Mia's nervous gaze.

The policeman grabbed my wrists, tugged them behind my

back, and clasped cuffs on them. I shook my head, still riled up, and tried explaining to the man behind me what had happened. That it wasn't my fault. That Mason was the one who had forcefully touched Mia.

But before I could explain my side of the story, the guy pushed me toward the door. The crowd parted for us, and I could see Mia out of the corner of my eye. Tears streamed down her cheeks, and she now buried her face into Serena's shoulder.

Was I ashamed about what had happened? Yes. Did I regret it? No.

Mason had needed a good ass-kicking. He needed to go to jail. He was as bad, if not worse, than Melissa's mother. Showing up to talk to Mia, following her into the restroom, touching her when she had been screaming at him not to.

The cop pushed me out of the building.

"It wasn't my fault. I'm not the one who should be in cuffs, heading to jail," I pleaded. "He touched her, groped her. You can ask anyone here. They all saw it."

"Sir, I'm going to need you to calm down," he said, gently pushing me against the side of his patrol car.

I shook my head. This night was over. We had been having one peaceful night. Mia was enjoying it. I was going to ask her that one question that would change both of our lives forever. And Mason had had to fucking wreck it.

"Do you have anything on you that could hurt me?" the man asked, patting down my upper body. He paused right before checking my pants pockets. "Anything in your pockets?"

My lips parted, and I looked around to see Mia and a group of people from the restaurant huddled close by. I looked down at the top of the car and lowered my voice, so nobody but me and him could hear it. "I have an engagement ring. Right pants pocket."

"An engagement ring?" he asked, voice a bit less tense. He

glanced toward the group of onlookers. "Is the lucky girl out here?"

"Yes," I whispered. "I'd appreciate it if she didn't see it."

The cop felt my left pocket, then my right, pulling out the ring box just enough for only me and him to see it. "We're going to need you to come down to the station for questioning."

"Am I under arrest?"

After glancing toward the crowd and seeing Mason being brought out in cuffs, the cop shook his head. "You're coming down for questioning until we can sort this all out."

"Sort it out now," I said through gritted teeth.

If I went all the way down to the station, this night would be even more ruined. There would be no salvaging it.

"If your story checks out, it shouldn't be long. I can safeguard the ring at the station or—I don't usually do this—I can let you keep it on you."

I pursed my lips, knowing that if they took it ... it'd be harder to keep from Mia. She'd come pick me up. She'd stand with me when I got my belongings. She'd see it and know something was up.

All I wanted was for her to be happy and for this night to be special for her.

"Leave it on me," I said. "It won't be long."

As a couple officers talked to Mia and the others, another cop pushed Mason into the back of a patrol car. I clenched my jaw, anger rushing through me. I had known exactly what I was doing when I went up in there and beat his ass. I had known I'd end up here, about to be put in the back of a police car by an officer, because I was protecting the person I loved.

But it hadn't mattered to me. I would do it again and again if I had to. Nobody touched Mia.

I glanced over to see Mia standing with Serena. Mia stared at me with pitiful, big eyes, her arms wrapped around her body. Tears raced down her cheeks, and all I wanted to do was go comfort her. He should've never laid his hands on her. I should be there, making sure she was okay after what happened.

"Let me go talk to her," I pleaded with the officer.

He pushed me into the back of the police car without another word, and I didn't refuse. Because while beating Mason's ass was to protect Mia and I knew I wouldn't get in any real trouble for it, refusing to obey a police officer could land me in jail. I could lose my job. Everything I had built for my family would be gone.

I rested my head on the back of the seat and blew out a breath through my nose. Adrenaline was still running through me, and when I saw Mason through the window, being taken out of the cop car and tended to by EMTs, I wanted to kick his ass again.

Maybe he'd take the fucking hint and finally stop harassing Mia.

# CHAPTER 32

MIA

*T*he patrol car disappeared down the road with Michael inside of it. When the officer had put him in the car, he'd refused to look out and look at me. I hurt because this was my fault. Michael was off to jail because of me. If I hadn't ...

I bit back my next few thoughts.

This wasn't my fault. It was Mason's.

I couldn't blame myself for Mason touching me, for Mason trying to force himself on me. I'd told him to stay away. I told him no. He was the one who hadn't listened, but hopefully, next time around, he would.

I tucked my face into Serena's side, tears streaming down my cheeks. Everything kept going to shit. Every time I turned around, something else happened, and I fucking hated it. I just wanted us to be happy together.

Serena rubbed my shoulders and guided me toward her car. Damien and Victor followed after us, Victor's entire body tense with anger. I knew he wanted another go at Mason, too, another chance to kick his ass after Michael did, but the restaurant had quickly kicked all of us out once the police got here.

"Come on, Mia," Serena said, pushing me into the car.

But I still couldn't think straight. I was a complete mess. I felt so violated and disgusted with myself. I didn't even know why. It was Mason's fault. I shouldn't have felt like this. I shouldn't have been touched. My lips parted, and I let out a whimper I hadn't even known I was holding inside of me.

Weak. That was all I was.

I couldn't even push him away from me.

Serena reached over me in the backseat and put on my seat belt, pulling my head against her chest. She stroked my hair and shushed me, telling me that everything was going to be okay and that Mason had finally gotten what he deserved.

Damien stepped on the gas and sped toward the police station as Victor balled and unballed his fists in the front seat. Jaw tense, he stared out the windshield and cursed under his breath.

I squinted through teary eyes, trying to get myself together. "I'm sorry for ruining the night," I said, grasping on to Serena. "I—"

"Stop it," she said. "You didn't ruin anything. Mason did."

"Why was that fucker even there?" Victor said. "I thought he wanted Melissa all to himself. He fucking has her, and now, he wants Mia back? What the fuck is his problem?" Victor looked back at me. "He's the fucking psychopath, Mia. Not you."

Damien stayed quiet in the driver's seat, focusing on getting us all there in one piece. But I could tell that he had something to say. Damien rarely got angry. He was always calm, cool, and collected ... but by the way his knuckles were paling on the steering wheel, I could tell that he was beyond furious.

After a fifteen-minute ride that seemed to last hours, Damien pulled up to the curb near the station to let us out. I hopped out of the car as soon as it came to a stop and hurried toward the door with Victor and Serena in tow.

"Michael Bryne," I said to the clerk at the front desk.

She typed his name into the system and looked back up at me. "He should be out shortly. They're just asking him a few questions."

I slammed my palms on the desk. "A few questions?! He did nothing wrong. He was protecting me from someone who wanted to rape me in the restroom," I said, voice shaky. Saying the words aloud made it seem so much more real. And a bad feeling in the pit of my stomach weighed me down.

It wouldn't have been the first time Mason had done something like that.

Last time he had … he had gaslighted me so much that I started to think that I wanted it, too, that I deserved to have him come home drunk in the middle of the night and start fondling my pussy while I was asleep.

"You're the woman he assaulted?" a police officer asked behind the clerk.

I wrapped my arms around myself and nodded.

"Would you like to press charges?"

Serena's eyes widened. "What kind of damn question is that?!"

Damien walked into the building and hurried over to us, resting his hand on Serena's shoulder. "Calm down, babe."

The officer looked at me, waiting patiently for my response. Serena was right. It was a stupid question. Of course I wanted Mason to pay for touching me so damn inappropriately. But I also knew the consequences of going up against someone with so much money. His family would try to deny it had happened, would bribe whoever they could to keep it on the down-low so Mason would still have chances to be successful, just like them.

But … I wasn't going to back down anymore. This wasn't only my life he was fucking with. It was my friends'. It was Melissa's. It was Michael's.

Serena rubbed my shoulders. "Babe, we'll be with you every step of the way."

I nodded at the officer. "Yes, I want to press charges."

After filling out some paperwork and answering some questions, I was instructed to wait in the lobby for Michael. Apparently, they were still questioning him about what had happened, but he wasn't talking until he had a lawyer, which, honestly, I was grateful for because Mason's lawyers would latch on to anything they needed to flip this on Michael. Make this his fault. Try to tear down his career because *Mason had touched me.*

After waiting for almost an hour, I caught an officer pushing Mason into the back. Before I could stop myself, I hurried back there and followed him. Not listening to the clerk telling me to wait in the lobby. Or my friends. Or anyone for that matter.

I couldn't hold back. Mason was not going to ruin our lives.

Someone caught my wrist, but I yanked myself away from them and pursed my lips as I saw Mason sitting in a holding cell. All I wanted to do was reach inside it and strangle him to death.

"Ma'am, you can't be back here," an officer said.

But I ignored him, knowing that I could get in trouble. I stepped toward Mason, my fingers curling around the metal bars.

"Don't you ever touch me again," I said. "Don't touch Melissa. Don't fucking touch Michael."

Or so help me God, I would kill him.

# CHAPTER 33

MIA

*A*fter another half hour, Michael walked into the lobby with a stack of papers and a black eye that was already swelling. I jumped up from my seat and wrapped my arms around his torso, pulling him toward me.

"I'm sorry that you're in this mess," I whispered. Part of me wanted to whisper to him not to hate me. Another part of me was scared that he'd see I was more trouble than I was worth to him. But I refused to let those insecurities appear right now.

This wasn't about me. This was about Michael.

A while ago, Victor and Damien had driven back to the restaurant to get Michael's car. I clutched the keys in one hand and took his in the other.

"I'll see you tomorrow," I said to Serena. "Thank you for coming down here."

She gave me a half-smile and shrugged. "That's what friends are for." After pulling me into a tight hug, she said, "I'll call

Melissa and tell her what happened. She deserves to know not to pick up his lousy ass from jail."

Victor tensed at the sound of her name. "Don't bother," he said, glancing at Michael, then back at her. "I already did."

My eyes widened. "You talked to her?"

"On our ride back," he said, sadness laced in his voice. "Didn't think she'd answer. I'll tell you about it tomorrow. Go home and get some rest." Victor gave Michael a tight smile and nodded.

I pulled Michael out of the building and toward our car. The entire ride back to our house, he didn't say two words as I drove. All he did was grasp my thigh and squeeze it every so often. My mind was reeling with so many questions and thoughts. I didn't know what to even say to him.

So, I didn't say anything until we reached home. I opened the front door for us and pushed him toward the living room, his swollen eye getting worse and worse by the minute. It was a purplish-black color, the eye itself almost entirely closed.

"Sit down. I'm going to go get something to clean you up."

After retrieving a wet towel, some bandages, and other medical supplies from the upstairs bathroom, I walked downstairs and saw Michael sitting on the couch, leaning over his legs, chewing on the inside of his lip.

Nervous.

I sat down on the couch beside him, touched my fingers to his chin, and lifted it. "Let me see," I said.

My heart ached so bad for him. He must've been hurting himself. The bruise looked so bad.

I stared at his swollen eye and gently cleaned off his face with the wet towel, getting rid of any trace of blood. He winced when I drew the rag against it, and I pulled away almost immediately.

"Sorry," I whispered.

"It's okay." He rested his hand on my thigh, rubbing his fingers in soothing circles against my skin. "Continue."

I wiped off the blood, feeling Michael's gaze all over my face. When I finished, I excused myself to grab an ice pack from the fridge. My throat felt tight, and I wanted to cry again because what had happened to Michael was my fault. But I knew he'd tell me it wasn't.

When I returned from the kitchen, Michael sat on the couch with an unreadable expression on his face. It looked to be a mixture of worry and uneasiness and fear. I sat down beside him again and placed the ice pack on his eye.

He watched me, focus traveling around my entire face.

I gave him a tense smile. "So—"

"Don't," he said before I could even finish. "It wasn't your fault, and you're not taking the blame for it. I would do it again if I had to. I'd do anything for you." He paused for a moment, placed the ice pack on the coffee table, and grabbed my hands. "I planned for this night to be special for you—for us—but every time I want it to be, something always fucks it up."

I frowned at him and went to brush a strand of hair off his forehead, but he held my hands tighter.

"These past few months, you have shown me what real strength is. I love every piece of you—the way you smile, your laugh, your tears, your resilience. I have fallen completely for you, Mia."

My heart raced, my entire body feeling so warm and bubbly. Despite how disgusting I'd felt earlier, Michael seemed to wash it all away. He always made my life better, could always make me smile, make me laugh, make me feel as if a man could really and truly care for me, even in my darkest times.

He pushed his hand into his pocket, pulled out a small leather box, and knelt on one knee. My heart pounded even harder.

He took my hand. "Marry me, Mia."

# CHAPTER 34

MIA

*I* stared down at him, then at the ring. Oh my God ... Michael was asking me to marry him. This wasn't real. I must be dreaming. This whole night must've been one big dream.

"Michael," I whispered, grinning, "are you serious?"

"Yes, Mia," he said, clutching my hand. "I want to marry you."

Overcome with so many emotions, I choked out a raspy, "Yes!" I flung myself into his arms, nearly knocking him down, and wrapped my arms so tightly around his neck, refusing to let go. "Oh my God. Yes. Yes. Yes. Yes. Yes!"

He chuckled into my hair and pulled me tighter, standing up with me in his arms. When I finally pulled away just enough, he grabbed my hand and pushed the ring right onto my left ring finger. I stared at it in awe, then at him with love.

My heart pounded in my chest. This was real. Michael had proposed to *me*. I hugged him so close again.

"Now, as long as you don't mind a man with a bruised eye

taking you to bed, I'd rather finish this night on a better note." He grabbed my waist and pulled me closer, kissing him.

I wrapped my arms around his shoulders, pressed my breasts against his chest, and kissed him back—hard. "I don't mind," I whispered against him.

Picking me up, he walked toward the bedroom, cradled the back of my head in his hand, and laid me on the bed. His lips moved from my mouth down the column of my neck, leaving hot and needy kisses. I ran my hands all over his body, tugging his shirt over his head and kicking off his pants.

He continued to kiss down my body, between my breasts, down my abdomen, up my inner thighs, taking off all my clothes in the process. Lying between my legs, he dipped his head and placed his hot mouth on my pussy. I interlocked my fingers with his, and he started to leisurely eat me out.

My back arched, and I grasped his fingers tighter. Delight rushed through my body as the tension built in my pussy. I moaned out as his tongue moved in circles around my clit.

"Michael," I whispered.

He pushed a finger inside of me, then another. My pussy tightened around them.

"Michael, please, I need you."

He kissed back up my body, sucking on my nipple and grabbing my tits. I tightened when the head of his cock brushed against my aching pussy. He pressed his lips to mine in one lingering kiss, then pulled away.

"Please," I begged, needing him more than anything.

He rested his forehead against mine and slowly pushed himself inside of me. I wrapped my arms around his neck and pulled him toward me. As soon as I kissed him, he pumped in and out. His lips devouring mine. His tongue slipping into my mouth.

When he pulled away, he sucked on the skin below my ear. "Mrs. Mia Bryne," Michael whispered against my neck, letting me hear the name for the first time.

My pussy gripped around his cock, and I moaned into his ear. "Do you like the sound of that?"

I gulped and nodded, the pressure driving me even higher. "Oh God, Michael. Say it again," I said, digging my nails into his back. I wanted to hear it over and over and over.

"Mrs. Bryne," he whispered, thrusting into me.

His hips hit mine, his cock pounded deep inside of me, and my walls clung around him. The force built stronger and stronger in my core until I felt like I was about to explode.

I furrowed my brows and clenched. "Michael, I'm gonna … I'm gonna …"

He stuffed his face back into the crook of my neck, pressed his lips just below my ear, and sucked on my skin again. His body tensed, and I could feel his cock throbbing inside of me, filling me with his cum. I cried out, my body trembling against his, my walls pounding around his cock.

My body tingled in delight, pleasure pulsing through me. He sat up on the bed, keeping his arms around my body, his cock still buried inside of me. I could feel his cum dripping down my thighs.

"You're all mine, Mia."

# CHAPTER 35

MIA

The next morning, I rolled over in bed to rest my head on Michael's chest and opened my eyes to the blazing morning sun. I lifted my hand to make sure I still had the ring on my finger and that everything that had happened last night wasn't a dream.

But there it was, a cushion cut diamond, glistening so brightly on my finger.

My heart warmed, and for once in my life, I felt loved. All the men before Michael had let me down. But since the moment I'd met him, I hadn't felt that way once. He was always there to try to make me a better person, to make me happier. A day didn't go by when I didn't appreciate this man.

Michael's chest rumbled, and I glanced up at him to see him chuckling at me. "Good morning."

I poked his stomach. "What're you laughing at?"

He wrapped his arms around me, pulled me tight to his chest, and smiled brightly at me. "Nothing." His grin widened. "I just can't wait to spend my life with you."

I mirrored his grin, swept my fingers over his swollen eye, and furrowed my brow at him. "Does it hurt?"

"Like hell."

"Do you want me to get you another ice pack?" I asked.

"Not now. Maybe after my shower." He grasped my chin in his hand. "How are you feeling after last night at the restaurant? I never got a chance to ask you."

My lips turned into a frown as I thought about Mason. I knew I had a long journey ahead of me, trying to get him to pay for doing that to me. Mason came from money, and money usually meant no consequences—at least, around here.

"I'm fine. I don't want to think about it right now. I hate him." I tapped my fingers against his bare chest. "Let's talk about something else, like going to see my mom! Can we go today?" I cheesed up at his perfect fucking face. "Pleeeease. I wanna tell her about us."

"Of course we can."

As soon as the words left his mouth, I grabbed my phone from the nightstand.

**Me: Meet me at St. Barbars ASAP!!!**

**Serena: OMG, what happened?! Is it your mom again?**

When I didn't respond in 0.0003 seconds, the phone buzzed again.

**Serena: Mia! What happened? Is it serious???**

I grinned and swung my legs back and forth.

**Me: Kinda serious, but not bad. <3 Plz come. You'll love it.**

Michael chuckled from under me. "You haven't told her yet?"

I raised a brow up at him. "I didn't have time last night. Someone wouldn't let me leave the bedroom."

After we showered, Michael drove us to St. Barbars as I held an ice pack to his face despite him telling me not to. I wanted the swelling to go down. He would have to go to work like this on Monday morning.

When we checked into St. Barbars, Carol gave us a tense smile. I stuck Michael's name tag right on his chest, letting my left hand linger there, my heart filling with so many butterflies when I saw the ring again.

I must've stared at it for so long last night. I just … I couldn't believe that I was engaged to him. It was really real. It'd happened so soon, but everything always felt so right with Michael. We had gotten through everything I could ever even imagine, and we had come out stronger.

Michael grabbed my hand and walked with me toward Mom's room. I rested my head on his shoulder as we walked down the hallway, hand in hand.

*How will Mom and Serena react when I tell them? Hopefully well.*

When we walked into the room, Serena sat with Mom, looking as if she'd sprinted there. Victor and Damien were talking with James in the corner of the room. Mom gave me a look, eyes wide.

"Oh my gosh," Serena said, staring wide-eyed at Michael's black eye. She frowned at him and glanced between us. "This sucks … but at least Mason will be sitting in jail for a bit longer for what he did."

"Michael," Mom said, shocked. "What happened to you?"

"Long story," Michael said, "that I think we'd all rather not get into right now."

Serena nudged Mom. "I'll give you the deets later. Let's just say, Mason is an asshole."

Mom nodded, a pained expression on her face, then turned back to me. "Is this what you wanted to tell us, sweetie? Serena made it sound like you had some *good news* to let us all in on."

I glanced up at Michael and grinned. God, this was really happening. After looking back at my family and friends, I pushed my hand toward them and smiled even wider, which I hadn't even thought was possible.

"OH MY GOD!" Serena leaped up from her seat, snatched my hand, and pulled it close to her face, as if she couldn't believe I was engaged.

*Engaged* ... it sounded so weird to even think.

"Oh my God!" Serena pulled me into a hug and jumped up and down, spinning me around with her. "My best friend is getting married!"

Mom grinned at me as if she had known this entire time what Michael was up to behind my back, plotting a proposal. "Only had to get a black eye before it happened," Mom said to Michael, giving him a wink.

Mom pushed herself toward me and pulled me into a hug. "I'm so happy for you. You don't know how hard it has been to keep this to myself for the past week. I've almost slipped so many times."

"You knew about this?" I asked.

"Yes! Michael came by a while ago," she said, smiling at him.

"Okay, serious question." Serena glanced playfully over at Damien. "We've been dating for five years," Serena said, wiggling her fingers in the air and letting out a giggle. "Where's mine?"

# CHAPTER 36

MIA

"Faster, baby," Michael said, placing his hands on my hips and moving them back and forth for me.

I curled my fingers into his taut chest and moved my hips with his, loving the feeling of him inside of me.

We had stayed almost the entire day at St. Barbars, celebrating with my friends and family and visiting Mr. Bryne, who was as happy for Michael as Mom had been for me. We had taken him out to the garden and to meet Mom for the first time, picked oranges from the orange tree out back, and told him about why Michael had a black eye, to which he responded with a curt, "Good."

And now … we were back at home with the sun setting over the trees. I threw my head back, feeling Michael's thumb slip between my legs, rubbing small circles over my clit.

Today was one of the best days of my life. I'd never thought I'd have something like this happen to me—to be in a relationship with someone who actually cared about me and wanted to be with me *and only me* forever.

Michael pulled me down to him, sucked one of my nipples into his mouth, and started to fuck me until my pussy was pulsing on his cock.

"Oh God, Michael," I breathed out into his ear. The pressure built higher inside me. "Please don't stop."

He wrapped his arms around my torso and pounded deeper and faster into my pussy, refusing to stop. His teeth grazed against my nipple, and my entire body was flooded with pleasure. It rippled through me and warmed my core.

Michael grunted and stilled, coming deep inside my pussy until I was full with his cum. He pulled out slowly and let me roll off him as he tried to catch his breath. "Damn, Mia," he said, his chest rising and falling, and covered with sweat.

I buried my face into his shoulder and smiled against him, feeling so damn good. I brushed a strand of his hair from his face and looked up at him. "I want a fall wedding."

He smiled and parted his full, swollen lips. "Fall is close," he said. "A couple months away."

"Is that too soon?" I asked, staring into his gray eyes. "I thought it'd be a good, refreshing start for me. I'll be starting grad school, getting everything back on track," I said. "I think it'd be perfect."

"You're going to have to pick out a dress soon and help me plan. Are you up for that?" he asked.

I frantically nodded, not having been more ready for anything in my entire life.

Wrapping his hand into my hair, he pulled me closer and pressed his lips to my forehead. "If you want a fall wedding, then we will have a fall wedding, Mia. Anything for you."

# CHAPTER 37

MIA

The next morning, I woke up early and tried to get some schoolwork done in the kitchen as Michael slept. I was so close to finishing, and I couldn't wait to get it over with and start grad school. Undergrad had been shit for me.

Someone knocked on the door, and I froze in my seat. The last time this had happened, I had been met with an angry ex-wife, who turned into a crazy piece of—

They knocked again, and I glanced down the stairs to see Melissa in the window.

I stared at her for a few moments and gulped. She didn't know that we were engaged, did she? What would she say when she found out? Was she—

She waved to me through the window and gave me a half-smile. I took a deep breath, ran down the stairs, and opened the door.

"Michael is sleeping," I said, not sure what else to say to her. Part of me wanted to despise her for staying with Mason after all this—especially after what had happened to Michael—but the other part of me felt sorry for her.

"I actually came here to talk to you." She glanced inside. "Can I come in?" When I opened the door wider for her, she walked in and took off her shoes at the door. "Can we talk?"

I followed her into the other room, heart racing in my chest. How did I tell her we were engaged? Should I be the one to tell her, or should Michael? She was *his* daughter ... and I was going to be her stepmother. My eyes widened at how weird it sounded. Melissa used to be my best friend, and I was going to be part of her family now.

Instead of sitting down on the couch, she went out by the pool and dipped her feet into the water. I sat a few feet away from her and kicked my legs back and forth. We sat there in complete silence in the scorching sun until she spoke up.

"I wanted to apologize for everything. I shouldn't have done anything with Mason, and I really shouldn't have reacted the way I did when you warned me about him, especially when you were going through everything with your mother."

My heart hurt, and I watched the water ripple around my toes. "Are you still seeing him?"

She paused for a long moment. "No. I broke it off with him after what he did to you."

I glanced up. "After what he did to me?"

She looked me right in the eye, her gaze faltering for a moment, and then she steadied it. "After he tried to force you into sex at that restaurant. He wanted me to bail him out, but when I found out what he did, I refused."

Tears welled up in her eyes, and she shook her head. "I'm sorry I didn't see it sooner. I'm a terrible friend. I should've listened to you. I just ... I'm pre—"

"Melissa, I know. It's ok—"

She wiped her tears with the back of her hand. "No, it's not okay. I went to my mom because I was angry with you for sleeping with my dad. She spread rumors about you that I knew weren't true. I was a bitch about this whole fucking thing, and now, you and he will pay for it for the rest of your lives. I've destroyed your lives. You'll always be looked at as *that* couple."

I scooted closer to her. Everything she'd said was true, and while I didn't want to give in to her and tell her everything was all right, I knew she was hurting badly. Maybe being nice to people was going to destroy me one day, but I didn't want to be rude.

She might've deserved backtalk, but it didn't make me feel good. I had done some pretty shitty things too.

So, I wrapped my arm around her and pushed my feelings aside. She rested her head on my shoulder.

"I'm sorry, Mia. I'm so sorry. I was jealous. I didn't want you to take him away from me. I've completely freaking crushed your life completely."

"You didn't ruin my life." Maybe made it a lot more difficult, but not *ruined*.

Michael wouldn't let anything wreck us, and I was so fucking happy about that. I had a man who'd be here for me through everything.

After a few moments, I pulled away and rested my hands in my lap, rubbing them against my sweaty thighs.

Melissa glanced down with wide eyes. "He proposed to you?"

My heart raced again, and I hesitantly nodded. While I expected her to flip out, to call me some kind of name, or to blame me for the falling-out between her and her father, she smiled tensely and nodded back to me.

"He told me he wanted to spend his life with you."

"He did?"

"Yes." She glanced down, then back up. "He's a really good person, Mia. I don't want to see him hurt again. After what happened with my mom, he was a complete mess. He deserves to be happy ..." She paused. "And so do you."

I sat there in disbelief. Melissa wasn't throwing a fit about this, and for the first time in a long time, I thought that maybe we could be friends again—real and true friends. Nothing would be the same between us, but we could still do things together. And hopefully, this pregnancy would calm Melissa the party girl down a bit and ground her in reality.

After sitting for a few moments in silence, I inched closer to her. "Do you want to go dress shopping with me, my mom, and Serena on Saturday morning?" I asked, hoping to lighten the mood. I didn't know how she'd respond or what she'd say, but I wanted her to feel okay with me again.

"I have to work Saturday morning," she said, the corner of her lips turning down. She paused, as if she didn't know what she should say next, but then she said, "But I'm free later on. We could go out to eat after your day of shopping?"

A smile found its way onto my lips, and I nodded. "That would be perfect."

Michael walked out onto the deck with a cup of coffee and leaned over it, dressed only in a pair of sweatpants. "Melissa," he said, taken aback when he saw us. "I didn't know you were coming over."

"Oh my God," Melissa whispered, tears forming in her eyes. She stood up and hurried over to the deck, staring up at him and his swollen black eye. "Did Mason do that to you?" She parted her lips and pressed them back together, as if she had more to say but didn't know *what* to say or *how* to say it.

Michael grimaced and nodded inside. I hopped up from the pool and followed Melissa into the house and up to the kitchen.

"What do you girls feel like eating?" he asked, pulling out pancake and waffle mix.

"Dad," Melissa said, shaking her head and stopping him. "Did Mason do that to you?"

Michael looked at me, then back at her. "Yes."

From the look on his face, I could tell that he was torn on

what to say next. He had told me that he tried to get it through Melissa's head that Mason was no good and that she didn't care. He probably didn't want to waste his breath, trying again.

A tear slid down her cheek, and she collapsed into one of the chairs with her head in her hands. "I hate him so much," she said, voice trembling.

I grabbed the box from Michael and nudged him over to her.

"I can't believe how big of a fool I've been."

Michael sat next to her and cleared his throat. "I love you, Melissa, but I need you to know that he's not welcome here. Not after what he tried to do to Mia. I don't want him in this house —ever."

Melissa wiped the tears away with the back of her hand. "I broke up with him."

Michael froze. "You broke up with him?"

She nodded, and I gave Michael the smallest smile. As bad as it sounded, that black eye wasn't for nothing. It'd solidified how shitty Mason was and how terribly he'd treat Melissa if she stayed with him.

"After what Victor told me that he did to Mia"—she shook her head—"I couldn't stay."

Michael sat up taller, and I started the stove, pouring the pancake mix and ingredients into a bowl, then onto the skillet.

"Are you moving back?" he asked, so much hope in his voice.

"I'm gonna stay with Serena for a bit. She said I could until I found somewhere."

"Stay here," I said, looking back at her and setting the mix onto the skillet.

She glanced between us and shook her head. "I know you both want me to, but I ... I need to take some time by myself. I want to know that I can do things without Mason or Victor or you, Dad." Michael went to say something, but Melissa started again. "Once I'm further along in my pregnancy, I'll think about coming back here. But right now, I need some more time. And you two should spend some time together, too, seeing as you're engaged now."

Michael looked at me and smiled, then grasped Melissa's hand. "Promise me that you'll come back if you need anything during the pregnancy. Your room is always open." He ruffled her hair like I remembered him doing when we were younger. "And I'm glad you got yourself out of that mess."

# CHAPTER 38

MIA

*M*onday morning, I sat in class with a huge grin on my face. Undergrad might've been shitty, but I was glad it'd be ending in a few weeks. Everything seemed to be coming together slowly but surely.

"Mia," Dr. Xiao said before class ended. "Please come speak with me after class."

After she dismissed the class, I closed my laptop and stuffed it into my backpack, lingering behind until everyone left the room. I walked up to her desk and smiled.

"Is everything okay?" I asked.

"You're smiling, dear," she said, eyes lit with happiness. She placed her laptop into her bag and looked over at me. "You haven't smiled for this long since I met you."

My heart warmed, and I nodded. "Everything's finally… good," I said. "With my mom and Michael." I held a hand to my heart, fingers digging into my chest lightly. Now, all I had to deal with was school, and I'd be back on track.

Dr. Xiao's eyes widened, and she took my hand. "Mia, you're engaged?" she asked.

My cheeks flushed, and she clapped her hands together.

"That's amazing!" She reached into her bag and pulled out a folder, looking through it. "And I hope to bring you other good news too."

She handed me a sheet of paper that had a bunch of information about her graduate school office hours and the lab internship she oversaw.

I furrowed my brows down at it. "What's this?"

"I saw your application for grad school," she said. "And I saw that you were still looking for a paid internship position. Luckily, someone dropped, and I have space for you in my lab."

*Is she serious?* She was really offering me a spot in her lab, which was one of the most difficult to get into in the entire psychology graduate program.

"Are you serious?" I asked breathlessly.

After nodding, she grinned at me. "I'd love it if you joined us. You're one of the hardest-working students I've seen come through the undergrad program. It would be twenty hours a week, and you'll be paid higher than minimum wage while gaining some quality experience."

Tears welled up in my eyes, a single one falling down my cheek, and I swept one away. "Thank you," I whispered.

She wrapped one arm around my shoulders. "Oh, Mia, don't cry. You should be proud of yourself. I know I'm proud of you, and I bet your mother and Michael are proud of all you've done too."

Overcome with so much happiness, I let another tear fall and nodded. I was proud of everything I'd accomplished. There was so much at this moment that I was grateful for. I'd never thought I'd be here.

"Only a month left to go until graduation," she said, hanging her bag over her shoulder.

One month. One freaking month, and I would be finished with undergrad, only a semester longer than planned.

"You got this."

I nodded and walked out of the room with a smile on my face and a huge weight off my shoulders. I had gotten accepted to one of the best psychology programs in the country, was going to intern in the lab that I'd been dying to work in for four years, I was freaking engaged to the man of my dreams, and Mom was better. So much better.

*  *  *

I MUST'VE BEEN in a better mood than usual because Sal almost immediately noticed.

"What's got you all happy today?" he asked, sitting in front of me at the bar and stuffing a pen into his pocket. "You never smile this much."

Placing his favorite drink in front of him—a Sprite—I grabbed a rag and washed the bar top. "Just some things," I started. "Some reall—"

Sal grabbed my hand. "What's this?" he asked, looking at my hand. "That boy didn't." He slapped the countertop. "Michael proposed to you, didn't he?" Before I could even get a word into the conversation, Sal continued, "See, I saw the way he was looking at you the other night. I went home to my wife and said that you two would be engaged by the end of the month. And looky!"

A laugh escaped my lips, and I let him look at the ring. "That's not the only good news," I said.

"Are you pregnant too?" Sal asked.

"No," I said, shaking my head. "Definitely not pregnant."

I gnawed on the inside of my cheek at the thought of having kids with Michael. I didn't know when I'd want to have them, but

… did he even want to have kids? He *was* older than me and had Melissa already. Would he want to raise another one?

"Then, what the hell is it?" Sal asked.

"I found out today that I'll be participating in an internship in the fall," I said to Sal.

It might not be good news to him since I was going to have to stop working here. But it was great news to me.

I toyed with the ends of the rag. "So … I won't be able to work here anymore, starting in September."

Sal let out an exasperated sigh and shook his head. "It's about damn time."

"You're not angry?" I asked.

Sal leaned against the bar and started laughing in the *crazy old man* kind of way. "No, Mia! You've been here for years. It's about time you started focusing on yourself and not entertaining other boys in this bar. You have your whole life ahead of you. You'd better be visiting me with Michael. Bring him around more often. I miss him here."

He tapped the counter with the side of his fists and got up from his seat. "Oh, and Mia? I'd better be invited to the wedding," he said, chuckling away as he walked toward one of the back rooms. "Or I'll be after Michael for that one."

# CHAPTER 39

MIA

*S*aturday morning, I sat on the edge of the bed and clutched my belly, my head in my other hand. Light flowed in through the window, and I moaned quietly in pain, trying not to wake Michael up because it was his day off.

My stomach tightened, and I felt like I was about to puke my guts out. I squeezed my eyes closed, hoping the feeling would pass quickly because I had to go dress shopping today. We had already made an appointment, Serena had taken off work, and I wanted to go.

When I gagged, I hurried to the bathroom, stuck my head into the toilet, and vomited. It was quick, but I felt like shit the entire time. I flushed it down and cleaned my teeth, hopping into the shower before Serena picked me up in Damien's car so we could get Mom from St. Barbars.

When I came out, Michael sat in his bed, scrolling through his phone, chest bare to me. He looked up and furrowed his brows.

"Did you get sick this morning?" he asked, placing the phone down next to him.

"Yeah, but I feel better," I said, brushing it off as if it were nothing. "It was probably that chicken last night at the restaurant."

He paused, giving me that hard expression he always did when he wanted to say something, but then nodded. "You okay to go out today? You can always reschedule," he said.

I kissed him on the lips, heard Serena blast the horn outside, and said, "I'm fine. I'm going out with Melissa tonight anyway, so I can't miss it. I'll tell her that you love her." I swept my thumb across his lower lip and watched him smile. "See you tonight."

After kissing him again, I grabbed my things and hurried to Damien's SUV. Damien's father was handicapped, so this SUV was suitable for Mom's wheelchair and everything that she needed to go out with us.

We drove to St. Barbars, listening to music like we used to do. I held my stomach, vaguely feeling like I was about to puke again, and took a deep breath.

"Are you okay?" Serena asked as we pulled into the assisted living center's parking lot.

"I'm fine. A bit nauseous. It'll pass."

Once I retrieved Mom from the building and put her into the backseat, we drove to the boutique downtown and parked on the side of the road.

"So ..." I smoothed out my shirt and pulled the door open to go into the bridal boutique.

Serena wheeled Mom into the store and stood at the front entrance with me, waiting for the woman to seat us.

"How's Melissa?" I asked Serena.

Mom looked up at her. "How is she? I haven't seen her in a long time."

Serena slapped my arm. "Why didn't you tell me that she was

157

pregnant? I found out the other day when she refused to have a glass of wine with me," she said.

Mom's eyes widened, a smile crossing her face. "Melissa is pregnant?! Oh my goodness!" She clapped her hands together and smiled wider at me. "Sweetheart, that means that—" She stopped herself short, her cheeks reddening.

When she didn't say anything for a few moments, Serena butted in, "Yeah, but it's Mason's." Serena frowned. "Have you heard?"

I rolled my eyes and groaned. Yes, I had heard about Mason. He'd sat in jail for a single night and been out by morning. From what Michael had told me, Mason had a court date sometime in a couple weeks. And I was praying that he'd get the maximum sentence he could get for sexual assault. But I highly doubted that he'd get half the maximum. He'd probably get more like paying a few thousand dollars in fines and a stern *don't do that again* by his father.

"He has a couple weeks," I said.

Serena rolled her eyes and groaned. "He shouldn't have been let out at all. He's disgusting."

A woman walked up to us with a big smile on her face. "Welcome to Adorn! I'm Rachel. Which one of you is the bride?" she asked, glancing between us three.

Mom pushed me toward her, and I awkwardly held out my hand and introduced myself.

"Well, Mia, we're going to find the perfect dress for you today."

She guided us to a couch, set out some wine for Serena and Mom, and led me to the back to start trying on dresses. After awkwardly standing in my underwear for ten minutes, she appeared in the doorway with five different dresses hanging across one arm.

After she handed me the first dress, I stepped into it and stared at my reflection with wide eyes. I was wearing a wedding dress … a freaking wedding dress. I, Mia, was going to be married to Michael Bryne.

Part of me didn't believe it. We had only been together for a few months, but it had seemed like lifetimes. I had so much love for him, and I knew that we could get through anything … but marriage was so sudden. And at the same time, I couldn't wait for it.

"So, who's the lucky man?" Rachel asked, zipping up the dress.

"His name's Michael," I said. "He's an architect, and he's such a sweetheart."

"Yeah?" she asked, placing her hand on my back and smiling at me through the mirror.

"He's so loving and caring and honest," I whispered, with Michael on my mind.

It made me smile, thinking about everything we'd been through and how it made us stronger. There'd be more drama, but we'd get through it.

"Well, Mia, I think he's going to love you in this dress." She opened the door for me. "Why don't we go see what your mom thinks of it?" She ushered me out into the other room, holding the train of my gown.

Mom sucked in a deep breath when she saw me, tears welling in her eyes. "My God, Mia." She fanned her face and squealed. "Mia, you look so beautiful! I can't believe that this is happening. My baby is getting married!"

# CHAPTER 40

MIA

*W*e had spent the majority of the morning at Adorn as I tried on dress after dress to find the perfect one. But none of the dresses fit me how I wanted ... until I tried on the last one. Sheer bodice, A-line style with a light V-neck. Slim around the waist and flowy from the hips down.

I felt like a princess.

A damn princess.

After I ordered the dress and got fitted for it, Serena and I brought Mom back to the assisted living center and went to Vinny's Pizza to meet Melissa. It was busy, but the waitress immediately found a booth for us.

There were a couple guys I recognized from Mason's frat in here, and I prayed to God that he didn't show up or that they didn't come over here to talk to us because either Serena or I would break and punch one of them straight in the nose.

"Do you think she'll come?" I asked Serena.

Melissa had gotten off work a half hour ago, and we were

supposed to be meeting her here for lunch, but she hadn't texted either of us all morning, which was unusual since she was *always* by her phone.

As the waitress came over to ask if we had anyone else joining us, Melissa squeezed past her and into the booth.

"Sorry I'm late." She looked up at the waitress and smiled. "Water, please."

Lunch went fairly quickly and smoothly with Melissa. She talked about her new job and how she'd been trying to save up enough to buy herself a new phone because—before all the Mason drama—he had thrown it and cracked it one night. I knew that Michael would buy her a new one in a heartbeat, but by the way Melissa had talked the other day, I thought that she wanted to do this all herself.

After we all finished off two large pizzas, Melissa pushed her plate to the center of the table. "I'm about two months," she said, her hand trailing over her small bump. "The first six weeks were terrible for me. I had so much morning sickness, all these cravings for pickles …" She scrunched up her nose. "I didn't even like pickles before this."

Serena glanced over at me and gave me a weird expression, then turned back to Melissa. "Are you sure that it's not Victor's?" Serena said. "You know that if it was, he'd step in and make sure that he or she had the best life. He's a good guy."

Melissa looked at the table and frowned. "He's a great guy," she said, sadness laced in her voice. A tear ran down her cheek. "I'm so stupid. I shouldn't have done what I did. I regret it every day." After wiping some more tears from her face, she looked at me with so much guilt. *I'm sorry*, she mouthed with tears in her eyes.

I gave her a half-smile. It still hurt part of me, but I couldn't care less about Mason. "It's fine," I said, grabbing her hand and squeezing gently. "I just want you to be healthy during the pregnancy, no matter whose it is."

She smiled, and then her phone buzzed on the table. For a split second, I thought it was going to be Mason, but it was an alert.

Melissa looked at it and frowned. "I have a doctor's appointment at three p.m.," she said. "So, I have to get going."

"Do you want us to come with you?" Serena asked.

"No. I asked my dad this morning," she said, smiling.

My heart warmed. Michael was probably over the moon about that. He'd definitely want to be there for Melissa as much as he could.

"I think it'll be nice to spend some time with him." After Melissa grabbed her things, she hurried to the exit.

When she was out of sight, Serena turned to me. "Are you pregnant?" she asked suddenly.

I stared at her with wide eyes and shook my head, in complete shock that she would even ask me. "You know I have an IUD." I had gotten it a year into my relationship with Mason, *not* ever wanting to get pregnant with his child.

She stared at me. "Hello? Morning sickness. Orange cravings. Refusing to drink alcohol. Nothing screams pregnant to me more than that. You heard Melissa."

Gnawing on the inside of my cheek, I shook my head. "I can't be pregnant," I whispered.

*But what if I really am pregnant?*

# CHAPTER 41

MIA

"Oh my God."

I stood in the bathroom with my pants at my ankles, blinking at the stupid pregnancy test like if I blinked so many times, the result would magically change. *No. No, this can't be happening.*

Serena banged on the door. "What does it say?"

Before she could barge into the room, I grabbed the other stick in the box and forced myself to pee on it. This isn't real. This can't be real.

*Please, please, please be fake.*

I didn't know if I could do this right now.

After standing, I paced around the bathroom, splashed water on my face, and tried to calm my racing heart. But it was no use as my breathing became ragged and my heart seemed to beat even faster.

*Lord, please, have a different result, please.*

But after the longest five minutes of my life, both tests read … *pregnant.*

I thrust my hand into the box for another stick, only to come up empty-handed. "Fuck."

Serena jiggled the doorknob and pushed the door open, catching me sitting on the toilet with my knees to my chest, clutching the two sticks in my shaky hand. She grabbed them from me, her eyes widening. "Pregnant."

My lips trembled. "What am I going to do?" I croaked out, my voice cracking.

What if Michael didn't want another kid? We hadn't even talked about it yet. I didn't think we needed to talk about it for a while, like *years.* Melissa was enough for him to handle right now, and he was so much older than me, and I had grad school, and what about—

"Calm down, Mia," Serena said, stroking my hair.

"What if he leaves me when I tell him?" I asked, wrapping my arms around myself. "We're not even married yet. We have been dating for a few months now, almost nearing half a year. I'm on birth control and everything."

Serena crouched down in front of me and grasped my knees gently. "When are you going to finally realize that Michael isn't going anywhere? He's not your dad. He's not Mason. He's a real man who'd do anything for you."

I knew that.

I knew he'd take responsibility for it. I just …

My lips parted, and I stared at her through teary eyes. "We haven't talked about having children."

"Well … that doesn't mean he's going to leave you when he finds out. Michael is responsible. He'll do whatever it takes— raise it, care for it, love it, just like he loves you." Serena pushed some hair out of my face and behind my ear. "Now, stop thinking like that."

I slowly peeled my arms away from myself. But it was more

than Michael. How was I supposed to raise a child? This summer, I'd finish college, and then I was going right into my master's training. I didn't have time to give birth and raise an entire child during all that. And Michael would have to work. He couldn't look after it.

And still, I was so young.

"Stop thinking the worst, Mia. If things get tough for you, you have your mom and James. Michael. You have me and Damien. Victor even. We're not going to treat you any differently, and we'll be there for you through everything."

My heart warmed, but I was still nervous. *How am I going to tell Michael that I am pregnant? Do I even want to keep it? Can I keep it?*

I clutched Serena's hand tightly and let a tear fall.

"You need to tell Michael as soon as possible," she said, pushing my tear away.

And as scared as I was, I knew I had to tell him sooner rather than later. I didn't know how far along I was. I didn't know anything about pregnancy, like what I'd have to do, what would happen—really happen—to me and my body.

"What about Melissa?" I whispered. "She's going to think that I copied her or that I'm trying to get all the attention, take her father's attention away from her."

I shook my head, not wanting more drama to arise between us. We were getting better together, and now that I was pregnant, like she was, things could get rocky again.

"Maybe I should get pregnant too," Serena said, wiggling her brows. "She can be mad at both of us."

I let out a small giggle and playfully rolled my eyes at her. "Stop it, Serena. This is serious. She's going to freaking hate me for this, and I didn't even mean to. I mean, I still have my IUD. I didn't even think I could get pregnant."

Serena sat down on the bathroom floor and gave me a hopeful smile. "You know there's always a chance of getting pregnant on any birth control. And besides, that IUD moves around, especially with the kind of sex you're having."

She threw me a wink, and I rubbed a hand over my face.

"Look, all I'm saying is that you have to tell Michael. I'm sure whatever you choose to do with it—abortion, adoption, keeping it—Michael will stay. And we'll all be here, supporting you."

I took a deep breath and shook my head, still not believing her that Melissa wouldn't freak out about it. She had admitted to getting jealous, and if these damn tests were right, Michael was going to be giving *me* the same amount of attention he'd give her during her pregnancy.

"Maybe this'll help you get closer to her again. You and Melissa can do all the pre-baby things you do, like exercise classes and birthing classes and, you know, stuff like that. Melissa isn't going to want to go alone, and she definitely won't ask Mason or Michael to go with her. It's a perfect time to patch things up with her."

After resting my forehead against hers, I let out a groan. I hadn't wanted this to happen at all. I hadn't wanted to be pregnant just when I thought things were going great. I didn't want this to ruin anything Michael and I had already. But deep down, part of me knew that nothing would be ruined between us.

Michael would be supportive, no matter what I chose to do.

At least, I hoped to God he would because I couldn't do this alone.

# CHAPTER 42

MIA

*W*ith the pregnancy tests stuffed into my purse, I took a deep breath and stepped into the house. I had stayed longer than I'd expected at Serena's house—crying, trying to convince myself that this was happening for the better, and figuring out how the hell I was going to tell Michael about this.

Michael's car was in the driveway. He had probably gotten home hours ago from the doctor's appointment with Melissa and was waiting to tell me how it was or even ask about my dress.

So many happy things we could talk about, and I had to break this news to him.

I cursed myself and shut the car door behind me as quietly as I could. *Think positive, Mia. Positive. Nothing you say or do is going to make him hate you. Nothing you say or do is going to make him run away from you either.*

After walking up the sidewalk and into the house, I bit my lip and closed the front door, my mind in a fog.

"There you are," Michael said, his hands sliding around my hips from behind. He buried his face into the crook of my neck and breathed in deeply. "I've been waiting for you to get back. Where've you been?"

My heart pounded in my chest. "At Serena's," I said a bit too quietly. To compose myself and to not seem suspicious at all, I forced a smile and turned my head in his direction. "I heard you went with Melissa to her doctor's appointment. How was it?"

"Good. The baby is healthy," he said, pressing a lingering kiss below my ear. "Now, tell me, *Mrs. Bryne*, what's the dress look like?"

Butterflies pulled in my stomach as I gently pushed him away. "It's bad luck to tell you anything about my dress before the wedding." I booped him on the nose and tried to smile as widely as I normally did.

Michael must've bought it because he pushed me closer to the wall, grinding his body against mine. "Tell me something," he said, his hot mouth all over me, his hands running all over my body, his stubble grazing against the side of my neck. "Come on, Mia. Anything."

"I, uh ..."

*Anything?*

He ran a hand over my stomach, and I froze. Literally tensed up. My lips parted, but no words would come out. All I wanted to say was that I was pregnant, but I couldn't speak. I thought that part of me still didn't even believe it.

Michael pulled himself away from me and cupped my face. "What's wrong?" he asked, gaze traveling all over my face to see if he could try to figure it out. "Are you ..."

*Pregnant! Yes, I am pregnant.*

*Goddammit, why can't I say it?* The words were stuck on the tip of my tongue, aching to be released but desperate to stay hidden so no drama would unfold after it happened. I just wanted to relax in peace for a few moments before my life became a disaster again.

"Having second thoughts?" he finished quietly, his voice filled with fear.

I shook my head. "No. God, no." I licked my dry lips. It was only two simple words that weren't all that simple for me to say after all. "I just …" I ran my fingers across his chest, and I closed my eyes. "Can we go get some ice cream or something? I've had a long day."

*Fuck.*

That wasn't what I'd meant.

Michael grasped my hands. He took my hand and led me to the car. "Anything for you."

\* \* \*

WE SAT across from each other, Michael watching me intently. I licked my ice cream as my heart raced in my chest.

*How am I going to tell Michael that I am pregnant? Does he want kids?* We hadn't even talked about this yet, and I was beyond nervous to hear his answer. *Am I ready for a kid? What if he wants me to get rid of—*

He grabbed my hand from across the table, skimming his thumb against my knuckles. "What's wrong?"

"Nothing," I said.

There was hurt in Michael's eyes, and I knew I'd screwed up again.

"When are you going to open up to me and tell me when something's wrong? We're in this together, Mia, for the long run."

*For the long run?*

I took a deep breath. We really were, yet I was still scared, and now, this time, I'd hurt Michael. He probably thought I didn't trust him or that I was hiding something. So, I parted my lips, about to tell him everything, when my phone started ringing in my purse.

Mom's ringtone.

My heart lurched, and I pulled my hand out of his—an excuse to prolong this conversation even more. I unzipped my purse to grab the call and stuck my hand into the pocketbook, fumbling around inside.

When I pulled the phone out, the pregnancy tests came with it, and I stopped breathing. *Oh my God. Why the fuck have I left them in here? What is wrong with me?*

I went to put them back into the bag as quickly as I could before Michael could see them, but it was too late.

He grabbed them from my hand, eyes growing wider by the moment. "What's this?" He stared down at them, knowing exactly what they were, and then glanced back up at me, lips parting in disbelief. "You're pregnant?" he whispered.

# CHAPTER 43

MIA

*I* parted my lips and pressed them back together about fifty times, not knowing what to say or how to say it. My ice cream dripped down my cone and onto my fingers, making them all sticky, but I couldn't seem to care. All I cared about was Michael and how he would take this news.

But I couldn't read his expression, didn't know if he was okay with it or not, which only made this shit worse. Usually, I could tell exactly what he was thinking—those gray eyes always gave him away. Not this time.

Tears filled my eyes, and my chin trembled, but I continued to stare at him. I silently nodded. "Yes," I whispered. "Yes … I'm pregnant."

I waited for him to say something. It felt like years before he even reacted, and I couldn't tell if he wanted this or not. He had a blank expression on his face, one that I had rarely seen before. His deep gray eyes seemed calm right now, not stormy, like they were when he was emotional.

When he didn't say anything, I grabbed the tests back from him and stuffed them into my purse. "Michael, I use an IUD for birth control. It has one of the highest protection percentages against pregnancy."

He grasped my hand. "What do you want to do?" he asked calmly. Too calmly.

"What do you want to do?" I asked, needing to know if he even wanted children.

"It's your body, Mia. You tell me."

I glanced down at my purse that held my tests, then back up at him, and sank further into my seat. "I don't know what I want to do, Michael. I'm scared. Things have just started to get better, and I don't want to screw them up. I want to be with you. I want to continue college. I want to be successful at my internship and job," I said. My heart raced. "But …"

"But?" he asked, eyes looking a bit more hopeful than they had been before.

Maybe he really did want this.

My chest tightened, my throat closing up. So many emotions were running through my mind, and I wondered how the hell I hadn't seen this earlier. The cravings. The morning sickness. I should've known. We would've had more time to figure stuff out.

"But I'd love to have a family with you," I whispered.

He grinned, and I had never seen more happiness in his eyes. "I want to have a family with you too," he whispered, knuckles brushing against my cheek. He grabbed a napkin from the center of the table and wiped the ice cream off my hand.

"You didn't seem too happy about it when you found out," I said, narrowing my eyes to make sure that this was what he wanted for real and he wasn't saying this because this was what I wanted.

He grabbed my hand and placed it over his heart, and I could feel it racing fast. "I wanted to make sure this was what you wanted. I don't want you to feel like you have to keep it for me. I know you're young and unsure, so I'll be content whether you decide to keep it or not. But if we keep it, I …" He grinned even wider. "I can't fucking wait, Mia."

My heart warmed, and I pulled him closer, pressing my lips to his from across the table, unable to hold myself back anymore. I was young, but I wanted a family with Michael. This baby was something I would have to think a lot about, but if I wanted to do it, I could. I knew I could. I just needed to make sure that this was what I wanted.

For once in my life, I could think about me.

"You have to think about school and your internship," Michael said to me. "It's a three-year program, and I'll parent as much as I can for you to complete it. We'll have to see how far along you are already. If your dress will still fit. If we need to move the wedding back. We—"

"Slow down," I said to him, realizing that there was a lot that I hadn't thought about yet. So many questions that I didn't have the answers to at the moment and so much uncertainty. "I need to make a doctor's appointment."

"We have to get the IUD out of you as soon as possible," Michael said. "I can see if Melissa's doctor has any openings, if you'd like me to."

I gnawed on the inside of my lip. "Melissa," I whispered. "I don't want her to get angry with me or you for this."

"Why would she get angry?" Michael asked me.

I arched a brow, wondering if he knew his daughter at all.

"When we were at the doctor's today, she told me that she wished she'd waited. You and she always used to talk about getting pregnant together, raising your children as best friends. Now, you can."

Now, we'd be raising them as aunts or uncles and nieces or nephews.

"You don't think she'll be angry?" I asked, hopeful.

If Melissa had really said that, she might not be as angry with

173

me for it. She might even enjoy doing all those *mommy* things with me. Maybe this could help us grow closer together.

Michael tossed my melting ice cream in the nearest trash can and lightly grabbed my chin. "Maybe she'll be annoyed at first, but she'll get over it. We can tell her Monday at the courthouse."

My eyes widened. "Monday? That's so soon. Do you think it'd be good to tell her way *after* Linda goes berserk at court for you wanting a restraining order, not before or even on the same day?" I asked.

Melissa planned to go with us to the courthouse on Monday, but adding *this* might make her think differently about everything.

"It's better to tell her sooner. I don't want either of you stressing out about this," Michael said, and then he started to dive into *everything* that we would have to do to prepare. It was almost as if he had been waiting for this moment for such a long time.

Michael cared. Michael loved. Michael would be the best damn father he could be.

And he already was.

# CHAPTER 44

MIA

*M*onday morning, I sat with Melissa behind Michael in the courthouse. Linda walked into the room with her head held high, her makeup done, and the strong stench of alcohol following her in. The judge looked up from her stand and arched a thick brown brow at her.

"Mr. Bryne," Judge Alkins said, shuffling some papers. "You're filing for a restraining order against Linda Brown, citing stalking as your sole reason."

Michael nodded. "Yes, ma'am."

Linda curled her fingers around her podium and gave Michael a pointed glare. "Your Honor, I've done no stalking, nothing that he's accusing me of. We just happen to be in the same places at the same times. Pure coincidence."

From the look on Michael's face, I could tell that he wanted to interject but didn't want the judge to get angry with him. Judge Alkins looked over at Michael, then back at Linda. She went to say something into her microphone when Linda started speaking again.

"All he does is lie. He's been doing it for years. Lying. Cheating on me when we were raising our daughter and with one of her own friends." She wiped fake tears from her cheek. "Do you know how it feels, knowing that your own husband would rather be intimate with someone underage than be with—"

"Stop lying," Melissa said, standing up next to me. Her voice was hoarse and full of hurt.

Everyone looked over to her, including Linda.

"You've lied about all of this. They were never in that kind of relationship when you were married or when she was underage, and you know it."

Linda looked at her, scrunched up her face in pure disgust, and shook her head. "My daughter doesn't know what she's saying. She's hormonal, delusional, and pregnant. She's nothing but a liar, like her father."

Widening her eyes, Melissa went to say something else, but I seized her wrist and told her to stay quiet. Fighting with her mother here wasn't going to make her feel better about herself. Linda was crazy and would do anything to make herself seem like an honest woman in the court of law.

She didn't care if what she lied about hurt her own daughter. All she cared about was herself.

I wrapped Melissa up in my arms and rested my head against hers. "It's okay, Melissa. Don't listen to a thing that she says. We know that she's lying. It doesn't matter what anyone else says or thinks."

"But—"

"Melissa," I whispered, stroking her hair. "It's okay. It's not the end of the world if some people think that."

I knew that now. The only people who mattered in our relationship were Michael and me. I didn't care who knew about us or what they thought about us. All I knew was that I loved that man who was trying to protect his growing family. And I would always love him. No matter what.

After the judge silenced Linda, she started asking Michael direct questions about the stalking and asked him to provide evidence. But Linda, being the bitch she was, continued to interrupt the hearing.

Less than ten minutes in, the judge shook her head and waved off some of the evidence that Michael had brought, as if she had already made her decision.

"Restraining order has been approved," the judge said, glancing over at Linda. "Ms. Brown, you will not have contact with Mr. Bryne. You will not harass Mr. Bryne, show up at his home, or follow his girlfriend to work to see him. If you do, there will be consequences."

Linda slammed her hand against the podium. "No, this is not fair."

"Life isn't fair, Ms. Brown. Please leave my courtroom. I don't want to hear this anymore."

When she refused to leave, a cop grabbed her by the arm and escorted her out of the room. Michael held his breath the entire time, and when she was finally gone, he looked back at me and smiled.

This shit was about to be over for good this time.

# CHAPTER 45

MIA

The Friday after the trial, Melissa sat in the waiting room with Michael and me, her knees bouncing up and down. I hadn't thought she'd ever be okay with this, and when I'd told her about my pregnancy, she'd had to take a moment to compose herself, but Melissa wasn't making a huge deal out of me being pregnant right alongside her.

She was here, supporting me, while I waited anxiously to get my IUD removed. I grasped Michael's hand and stared across the aisle toward Melissa, who gave me a weak smile.

"It'll be okay," she said.

"Mia," a nurse said from the doorway.

I stared at her and gnawed on the inside of my lip, standing up with Michael.

"Only patients back here, please."

Pressing my lips on his, I gave him a kiss and walked into the back, where they sat me in a bleak room.

"Okay, Mia. It says here that you're pregnant, which is your reason for removing your IUD. Is that correct?"

"I took a couple pregnancy tests from the pharmacy, yes."

She handed me a cup. "Let's have you pee in here, to be sure, and we can get you on your way."

After peeing in the cup, I placed it on the counter and walked back to the room with my heart racing. I wished that Michael or Melissa could've come back here with me. I would've been in such a better headspace. Doing this all alone was driving me crazy, especially with all this waiting.

The doctor walked back into the room with a smile on her face. "After testing your urine, I found that you are definitely pregnant. Congrats!" she said with a bit too much enthusiasm. "Now, as you must know, there's a twenty percent chance of a miscarriage when we take out the IUD, but it's essential that we take it out as soon as possible."

*Miscarriage.*

The word sounded so … so … scary.

My heart raced even faster. At that moment, I knew what I wanted to do. I wanted to have this child with Michael. I didn't want to lose it. I wanted us to be the happy family that we both had dreams about. All week, I had been going back and forth about what I should do, but now, I was more than certain.

I didn't want to lose this baby. I wanted to keep it, raise it, love it.

"Okay," I said quietly. "Please, take it out."

She instructed me to lie back on the bed and take off any clothing lower than my hips. I spread my legs, and she maneuvered something cold between them and stuck it right up my vagina to spread it apart. It hurt like hell, and I couldn't wait until this was over.

She shone a light into me and paused. "Hmm, that's weird."

"What's going on?" I asked in a breath.

She stuck two fingers up into me and wiggled them around,

touching my cervix. I jerked back and cringed, trying to hold myself steady.

"One sec, sweetie." She continued to wiggle her fingers around, and then she pulled them out completely and frowned. "I believe your IUD fell out, which is when you must've gotten pregnant."

"Fell out?" I asked, brows furrowed together in confusion.

"It rarely happens, but it can during intercourse or when you're using the toilet." She took off her gloves, washed her hands, and opened the door. "Let me run some tests before you leave, to make sure your baby is okay."

She led me to another room, put some gel on my stomach, and started an ultrasound, smiling away as a picture came up on the screen. I couldn't tell what she was looking at, but I found myself smiling with her too.

"Your baby seems healthy, Mia. Congrats."

My chest tightened up, and I had the urge to cry my eyes out. I was so overcome with happiness that I could barely hold it in. I pulled on my clothes and walked back into the waiting room to find Melissa and Michael.

"I'm keeping it," I whispered, wrapping my arms around his neck. "We're going to have a baby."

# PART 2

# CHAPTER 1

MIA

"Congrats, Mia," President Jacobbe said to me, shaking my hand onstage at my college graduation.

I grasped his hand in mine and smiled widely, feeling so damn proud of myself. This entire summer, I had been working my ass off to finish school, and while I wished I had finished on time, I wouldn't trade this for the world.

After walking offstage, I caught Michael sitting with Mom and my friends, and I blushed.

I had done it. I'd freaking done it. I'd made it through without Mason, without Dad, without an angry ex-wife after me.

I sat back down in my seat and watched the rest of the students receive their degrees. Since it was summer graduation, the ceremony was smaller than the spring commencement and finished much quicker. I picked out Dr. Xiao in the audience, sitting with some of the other students from her lab.

Though I wasn't officially a grad student yet, I'd started working in her lab about a week ago to get set up and understand how things worked around there. And it was a hell of a lot better than sitting in the house all day, horny as hell and waiting for Michael to come home from work.

I stared at President Jacobbe and placed a hand over my stomach, listening to him finish one of his speeches. A sweet craving for oranges hit me, and my stomach growled. Pregnancy had been tougher these past few weeks. Besides these cravings, I had been getting hornier than I ever had been before. All I could think about was Michael bending me over the bed later on and fucking me senseless in this damn cap and gown.

*Fucking weird, I know.*

But, God, it made me squeeze my knees together.

"Congratulations to our graduates. Please join us for some refreshments at the University Club," Jacobbe said.

Everyone started to disperse out of the auditorium and into the hallways, heading toward the University Club a few doors down.

Graduates stood for pictures at the entrance with their parents as I walked farther into the room. Dr. Xiao had a glass of wine in her hand, and when she saw me, she hurried over.

"Congrats, Mia!" Dr. Xiao said, throwing her arms around me and pulling me into a tight hug.

Behind her stood a few students from the grad program, who were chatting with each other.

At our university and this psych program, it was sort of a tradition to attend graduation for the undergrads. The psychology department always threw a grad party afterward. I had been to one in April when they graduated, and it was definitely worth attending for chatting and making connections with others in the field.

I held my degree close and thanked her. She ushered me toward the other students, and I excused myself to find Michael and get some water at the bar. My mouth was dry from sitting in that auditorium for the past two hours.

One of the lab assistants and grad students, Cameron, who had also been in Mason's frat last year, smiled at me. "Congrats, Mia. Officially a grad student." Cam nodded to the bar. "You want anything? The psych department saved up all year to get grads drunk off shitty wine."

After laughing, I shook my head and rested a hand on my stomach. "I'm good, thanks."

"I, uh …" He scratched the back of his head. "I heard you and Mason broke up."

Just at the sound of his name, I scrunched up my nose. I didn't even want to think about that man. He'd had his trial in court the other day, and I had avoided news about him at all costs, knowing deep down what his sentence would be.

"Yeah," I said, awkwardly standing beside him.

Michael caught my eye from across the room, where he stood, chatting up Dr. Xiao about something. He raised a brow, and I shook my head and turned my gaze back to Cam.

"We broke up a while ago."

Cam looked as if he wanted to say something but stopped himself. "I heard about what happened at the courthouse and wanted to apologize for what he did to you," he said just as awkwardly as I felt. "Brothers from *any* frat should act better than how he treated you. He should've gotten more than a slap on the wrist."

My heart dropped in my chest, and I stared up at him with wide eyes, promising myself that I wouldn't cry on the night of my graduation. "He didn't get any punishment?" I whispered, letting it sink in.

From the moment I'd pressed charges, I had known that nothing would happen to him because his parents had enough money to bribe anyone to look the other way. But knowing that there had been no justice broke my heart.

It felt like my entire world came crashing down. If Mason hadn't gotten any consequences, what if he tried to do something like that again to me or to someone else? I knew to stay as far away from him as I could, but another girl might fall for him like I had, get trapped in a relationship with him, and let him hurt her over and over.

Sometimes, abuse like that was difficult to get out of. People didn't understand how shitty an abuser could make you feel, like what he was saying was your fault, like you were the bad guy and deserved all the pain and suffering that he was giving you.

Cam grabbed my shoulder. "It sucks that guys like him can flaunt their money and get out of anything. If you need anything, you know where to find me," he said. "See you in the lab bright and early Monday morning." He threw me a smile and headed toward another group of grad students.

I grabbed a glass of water from the bar and hurried over to Michael, wrapping an arm around his waist and kissing him on the lips, trying to forget about Mason until a bit later when I knew I wouldn't burst out in tears.

Michael glanced over at the grad students, eyes lingering on Cam, and then he returned my kiss and pulled me closer to him. "I'm so proud of you."

"Thank God that's over," I said. "Because I'm about two seconds away from tearing off this gown and letting you give it to me right here. I didn't think I'd make it."

He placed his lips just below my ear and chuckled. "Wet for me again?" he asked into my ear, fingers curling around my waist.

"Always," I whispered to him, throwing him a smile.

I turned to Mom and my friends, waiting for the thousand and one pictures she'd want to take to remember this special day. And while I usually hated pictures, I wouldn't mind these ones. Today was a day I'd remember forever.

# CHAPTER 2

MIA

"So, I heard that Mason got off," I said, spilling the tea to everyone at the dinner following the after-party at a nice sit-down restaurant.

It wasn't that I was looking for any sort of reaction from them. I just couldn't hold it in any longer. After what Cam had told me earlier, my stomach had been in knots thinking about Mason. I didn't want to think what would happen if he got drunk like that again and followed an innocent person into the restroom.

"Are you serious?" Serena asked from across the table. She gave the biggest eye roll and sipped her wine. "That's ridiculous. I hate that freaking asshole." She glanced over at Melissa. "No offense."

"None taken," she said, placing a hand on her stomach.

But I could see that it did hurt her a lot. She either really loved Mason or didn't want to face the reality of him being the biggest asshole in our lives. I didn't know which it was, but it made me sad that she was in this alone and that Mason wanted nothing to do with her child. One day, she told me that she mentioned it to him, and he completely ignored it like it wasn't his problem.

He probably hadn't even told his parents about getting Melissa pregnant, not wanting them to disown him and refuse to give him money or support anymore. Mason thrived off his mommy and daddy's money. Take it away from him, and he was nothing.

"On the brighter side of things," Melissa said, steering the conversation elsewhere, "I went to the doctor's last Friday to find out the gender of my baby."

Michael almost choked on his wine. "Why didn't you tell anyone?"

Melissa smiled and glanced across the table at him, and then her eyes flickered to Victor, who sat across from her. Her eyes lingered for a moment, her teeth gnawing on the inside of her lip. Victor sat up in his seat, eyes on her.

"I wanted to wait until we were all together," Melissa said, gulping and peeling her gaze away from Victor.

I eyed the interaction and tried to hide the small smile creeping onto my face.

Victor still cared for her.

Yet it broke my heart to think about how Melissa's mistakes had broken him to pieces but that he still loved every bit of her. I didn't know if they'd ever go back to being together again. It was clear that there was something between them. But would we ever see a Victor-Melissa thing ever again?

I sipped my water. "Well, spill," I said. "What are you having?"

Melissa grinned. "A boy," she said.

Michael placed his hand on my thigh and squeezed lightly.

Mom clapped her hands together and leaned forward in her wheelchair. "That's wonderful, honey! When are you due?" Mom asked.

"December-ish," Melissa said with a laugh. "Actually, right before Christmas."

"Maybe you'll have a New Year's baby!" Serena said, clapping her hands together. "Ooh, that'd be so fun. Imagine having a baby the first day of the year before anyone else in the country."

All this baby talk was making butterflies flutter in my stomach. I was due at the end of January, which meant that Michael would get to spend some quality time with Melissa and her baby before ours came.

It was definitely weird, thinking about all of this, and I didn't think I'd ever be talking about baby stuff this close to graduating undergrad, but I was coming to enjoy it. I wanted to do some things still before the baby came—like getting married, the honeymoon, maybe even going to a party and dancing again, something simple so I could say that I hadn't missed out on any college experience even though I had.

Melissa started talking about getting a job at a nonprofit as my phone buzzed in my pocket. I pulled it out, trying to listen to the conversation, but when I saw the name and number on the screen, I froze.

**Dad: Congrats, Mia.**

I stared at my phone with wide eyes and furrowed brows. *Why the hell is he texting me? He hasn't wanted anything to do with me a few months ago when Mom was almost dying in the hospital. Why is he suddenly texting me now?*

After glancing across the table at Mom, I slid the phone in her direction. "Why is he messaging me?" I asked, hoping she had a reason even though I knew that she hadn't been in contact with Dad for years.

Mom read the message and rolled her eyes, pushing the phone back to me. "Because you're successful. He knows that you did this all by yourself, and he wants a piece of the pie." She frowned at me. "He's your father, but he's also a moocher. Don't let him think he's going to get anything out of you—not money or happiness."

I gnawed on the inside of my cheek and looked over at Michael, who frowned down at the message. The phone lit up again, and another message from him appeared.

**Dad: You should come over sometime.**

Mom arched a brow at the phone. "Is that him again?" she asked. After I nodded, she rolled her eyes. "Let me take care of him for you. You don't need the added stress of your father looking for more money to gamble away while you're pregnant."

But deep down, I knew that this wouldn't be the last time I heard from him. Mom was right. He was a moocher, and he'd try to get anything that I had, just to gamble it all away.

# CHAPTER 3

MIA

*T*he next week, in the grad lounge room—which seemed like everyone's own personal hell—I sat at my desk with a highlighter in one hand and a bunch of papers scattered in front of me. The day was almost over, and there were only a few grad students left here.

I helped around Dr. Xiao's cognitive lab sometimes, but most of my work so far had been research for my dissertation, which really meant sitting at a desk for hours, sorting through a bunch of research articles and daydreaming about Michael's hand around my neck as he pounded into me from behind.

His fingers digging into my hips. His cock pumping in and out of me. His—

"Mia?" Cam whistled from across the nearly empty room and cracked a smirk when I looked up at him. "Daydreaming again?"

My cheeks flushed, and I shook my head, trying to get back into these documents before I had to leave because once I left for the night, I wouldn't want to read any more about memory and cognition.

"No," I said, hoping that my mouth hadn't been hanging open as I thought about all the dirty things I'd make Michael do to me later. Because if Cam had seen that, I'd want to lock myself inside the house and refuse to ever come back here.

"Looks like you were," he said, chuckling.

"Trying to get through these articles," I said, hoping to steer this conversation elsewhere.

I glanced back down at the articles and blew out a deep breath. As much as I loved this stuff and wanted to learn more about it, some of these authors were so dry and boring.

Cam closed his laptop and walked over to me, placing one hand on the corner of my desk, the other on the back of my chair, leaning over to see the articles I had scattered all over my desk with sticky notes and highlighted pages. He snatched one from me. "First, don't murder the page with all this highlighting. It hurts *my* eyes, just looking at it."

I grabbed it from him. "But it's important."

He pointed to the bottom of the page, where I had highlighted a single word, and grinned. "*Is* seems very important," he joked. "You wanna tell me what deep meaning hides behind that word?"

After playfully rolling my eyes, I pushed the paper into my backpack. "Okay, maybe I need a break. I can't stand to stare at these articles anymore today."

Dr. Xiao walked into the room with a stack of papers. "You two are still here?" she asked, brow raised. She looked down at her watch. "I expected you to be gone fifteen minutes ago. It's already six forty-five."

*Shit.* Michael was waiting for me.

I pushed my notebooks and folders into my backpack and pulled it onto my shoulders, walking to the door, where Cam was waiting for me.

"What're you studying?" he asked as we walked down the halls to the exit.

I checked my phone, seeing Michael's name, and sent him a text, saying that I'd be out in a second. After putting my phone back into my pocket, I stared at the dirty floor in front of me. "Memory and amnesia. I was originally going to study aneurysms, but that's more neuroscience. Too much biology for my liking."

"Aneurysms?" Cam asked, pulling the door open for me.

"Yeah, my mom had two. In the spring, she lost her memory for a bit, so I thought it'd be good to understand it." I pulled my backpack higher up my shoulders as we walked through the quad to the parking lot. "What about you?"

"Cognitive neuroscience," he said. "Similar story as yours, I guess. My dad suffered a stroke when I was a freshman. I was on the business track, but I changed majors after seeing his recovery. It's not the same, but I'd like to know more about it."

I nodded and came to a stop when I spotted Michael's car in the opposite direction that we were walking. "Well, I'm this way," I said, nodding toward Michael.

"Cool. I'll see you tomorrow," Cam said, turning around to head for his car. He stopped in the middle of the parking lot and turned back to me. "Oh, I almost forgot. Some of the psych grad students from other labs are having a party Friday night. You're welcome to come."

For a frat boy turned grad student, Cam wasn't *anything* like Mason. And I was damn thankful because I wouldn't have been able to deal with being around him eight hours a day, five days a week. I would have probably gone insane. Cam at least had some manners.

I glanced at Michael, who sat in his car, tapping his fingers on the steering wheel and watching me. My core warmed, my cheeks warming at every single dirty thought I'd had all day today. God, I couldn't wait to go home with him.

Turning back to Cam, I smiled. "Um, I'll have to see what I'm doing. Maybe."

*Maybe not.*

"Let me know what you think." He slid into his car and shut the door, driving out of the parking lot and down the road.

# CHAPTER 4

MIA

Since my car had been at the mechanic since last week, I slid into Michael's passenger seat and rested my hand on the middle console, finally able to let out a nice, long sigh. "How was work?" I asked.

"Good," Michael said tensely, starting the car.

I arched a brow at him and waited patiently for him to continue because he definitely had more to say. After a few minutes of silence, he turned onto the main road.

"Who was that at your lab?" Michael asked, brow raised ever so slightly. "I saw you talking to him at your graduation too."

My gaze fell upon the windshield, and I frowned. "That's Cam. He's an assistant in Dr. Xiao's lab with me."

A few more tense and awkward moments passed, and then Michael cleared his throat. "I don't like the way he looks at you," he said, hand tightening on the steering wheel.

I rested my hand over my baby bump and looked over at Michael. A stubble on his tight jaw, eyes focused but firm, muscles flexing under his shirt. He glanced my way, and all the possessiveness faded for a brief moment.

"What?"

"Do you not trust me?" I asked, reaching over the middle compartment and resting my hand on his thigh as we sat at a red light. "Because all I could think about all day was you taking me the moment you came to get me. Me straddling your waist"—I let my hand drift up his thigh and over the growing bulge in his suit pants—"grinding my wet pussy against your cock."

Michael tightened his grip on the steering wheel to try to hold himself together. The light turned green, and he lightly stepped on the gas. "Mia," Michael said, yet he didn't push me away.

"What?" I asked, pulling out his cock and letting my thumb roll over the head of it. I didn't know what it was, but ever since a couple weeks ago, my horniness had turned up about a million notches. "I'm horny. Pull over."

Michael grew harder in my hand, and I started to stroke him, my hand tightening around his cock. Wetness pooled between my legs, and I ground my ass against the seat, clenching every time.

"Michael," I purred into his ear. "Please, pull over for me."

"We're in the middle of traffic," he said, licking his lips.

My lips curled into a smirk, and I leaned over the center console and dipped my head under his arm to suck his cock into my mouth. "Come on, Michael," I said, twirling my tongue around his swollen head. "Do it for me." I pushed him into my mouth until he hit the back of my throat. After pulling him out, I stared up at him through teary eyes. "I know you want to feel my pussy wrap around your cock, want my tits bouncing in your face as you fuck your fiancée senseless."

Michael groaned and placed a hand on the back of my head, stroking my hair as I took him back inside my mouth again. "Fuck, Mia …" He looked in the rearview mirror, pulling into the right lane, then turned onto a darker side street, parking the car on the side of the road.

When we were parked, I undid my seat belt, knelt on my seat, and leaned over to suck him off some more. Michael slid a hand under my shirt from behind and undid my bra, pulling it off me but leaving my shirt on. I opened my mouth wide for him and pushed him into me, inch by inch, until his cock hit the back of my throat again. I gagged on him, my eyes watering, and let him drive himself into me until I took every inch.

I could feel the bulge of his cock in my throat, and my cheeks flushed. I pulled my head back, trying to breathe, but he laced his fingers into my hair and held me in place, bucking his hips up.

My nipples stiffened against my shirt, and I leaned over even more as Michael slid his hand over my ass. He pulled my skirt up, pushed my panties down to my knees, and smacked my ass.

When his fingers slipped into my pussy, I bobbed my head quicker on his cock, my throat making sloppy, wet sounds for him. He wrapped his free hand around the front of my throat and tightened, starting to pump in and out of my mouth.

Spit dripped down my chin, and my breasts bounced against his thigh. All I could think about was him inside of me already, fucking me senseless. God, I wanted it more than anything.

After pulling him out of me, I pushed my underwear off and climbed into the driver's seat, straddling his waist. Michael grabbed my waist, teeth immediately latching onto one of my nipples in my shirt. He bit down softly, and I lowered myself onto him and moaned out loud.

His cock felt so big inside of me, and I couldn't help but dig my fingers into his shoulders. Michael pulled my shirt over my head, leaving me naked to him, and grasped my tits in his hands, his mouth all over them.

My pussy wrapped around his cock, and I bounced up and down, trying to relieve some tension between my legs. "Oh God,

Michael," I moaned. Pressure rose higher and higher in my core, about to send me over the edge soon.

Michael drove up into me and stared up into my eyes as he bit down on my nipple, sending a surge of pleasure through me. "Fuck, Mia," he mumbled against my tits, sucking on one.

I clenched tighter and ground myself on him, feeling so fucking good. "Come inside of me," I begged. "Please, Michael. God, I need it."

Michael wrapped his arms around my waist, pulling me closer to him, burying his face between my tits, and stared up at me, groaning. My pussy pulsed over and over and over on his cock, releasing my cum all over him until all I could feel was pure ecstasy.

I leaned back against the steering wheel and cupped his face. "I love you more than I love anyone in this world, Michael. Nobody is going to take me away from you and our growing family."

# CHAPTER 5

MIA

*A*fter lab the next day, Michael picked me up again and drove us to the doctor's office for a checkup. Today marked my sixteenth week as pregnant Mia, which meant that we might be able to find out the sex of our baby. Nothing was certain, but we were hoping we could.

My stomach was in knots the entire time, my knee bouncing wildly. Michael placed a hand on my thigh to calm me as he drove.

"What do you want to have?" he asked me, stopping at a red light.

I gnawed on the inside of my cheek and pursed my lip. To be honest, I hadn't thought much about the sex of the baby until the other day, when Melissa talked about hers. Whether it was a boy or a girl, I didn't really mind. But I could tell Michael was hoping for a boy, so I smiled at him.

"A boy," I said, watching him smile. "Have you decided on any names yet?"

We had gone through a whole bunch of them these past few weeks, though none of them felt right just yet. Maybe once we knew what we were having, it'd be easier to choose the name of the baby.

"Let's see what we're having first," Michael said, but he had that sly smile on his face that told me he had a few names in mind. Tapping his fingers on my inner thigh, he sent a wave of heat up it.

I pushed him away, knowing that we didn't have time to fool around in the car like we had yesterday. Because if we *had* had time, I'd have been ripping his clothes off already. Being horny was hard. But being pregnant and horny was even more difficult.

He pulled into the parking lot and found the closest spot to the entrance. "You know, I do have a couple boy names I like," he said.

I arched a brow at him and looped my arm around his as we walked to the door.

"Greyson or Easton, Harrison—"

I wrinkled my nose. "Harrison? Don't give our baby a fuckboy name."

He chuckled. "Fuckboy name?"

"I dated a Harrison in high school. Not a fan," I said, smiling up at him. "I like Easton."

Michael pulled the door open for me, and we walked up to the front desk.

"Hi, I have an appointment. Mia Stevenson," I said.

The woman gave me a clipboard with some information to fill out and told me a nurse would be with us shortly.

"Maybe Harrison could be his middle name?" Michael suggested once I finished filling out the papers on the clipboard.

I gave him a solid *definitely not* stare, to which he responded with a chuckle.

"Okay, Harrison is out."

"Mia," a nurse said, walking out one of the many doors.

Michael and I stood and followed her to the back room. My stomach was in knots as I went back and forth between a girl and a boy. Mom had told me that she knew for certain I was having a girl because I had been craving oranges, but I wasn't too sure about that.

At least, I was hoping there was a chance of it being a boy for Michael.

After the nurse got me situated on the bed and set up her machine and computer, she looked over at us.

"Do you want to know what you're having?" the doctor asked, smiling widely at Michael and me as she spread cold gel all over my stomach.

I glanced up at Michael, who raised his brows at me, giving me permission to do whatever I wanted.

Nodding eagerly up at her, I lay back on the bed. "Yes, please, we want to know."

After a few moments of setup, her monitor brightened, and we could see the ultrasound of the baby. She furrowed her brows for a moment, and then smiled.

"Ooh, so exciting! Congrats, you two. It's a boy," she said, pointing to the screen to show us.

My eyes lit up, and I intertwined my fingers with Michael's and squeezed tightly. *A boy? We are having a boy.* A bunch of new names raced through my head that we had picked out the other day because I wasn't one hundred percent set on naming our boy Easton yet.

Michael squeezed my shoulder and kissed me on the cheek, whispering into my ear about how excited he was for us. The doctor continued to point out the baby but paused mid-sentence. A look that I couldn't quite comprehend crossed her face.

"What's this?" she asked in a breathy whisper.

I gulped and sat up almost instinctively. "What is it?" I asked, thinking the worst. "What's going on?"

# CHAPTER 6

MIA

"Oh dear," the doctor said, staring at the monitor with wide eyes. She pulled out her stethoscope and placed it on my stomach, brows furrowed together. "I don't know how we missed this before."

My eyes widened, and I squeezed Michael's hand tighter.

"What's going on?" I asked, unable to deal with all the suspense. My heart raced in my chest, and I sucked on the inside of my cheek. "What's happening?"

It felt like the entire world slowed down, and all I could think about was the worst. *Has something happened to the baby? Is my IUD still inside of me? Is the baby not breathing? What the hell is it?*

The doctor tore off her stethoscope and placed it back around her neck. "Well …" she said, pausing. She sat back on her chair and pointed to the monitor. "Mia and Michael, it looks like you're having two boys."

My jaw dropped, and I sucked in a deep breath, glancing back over at Michael.

*What the hell does she mean, we are having two boys*?! I didn't even know if I could raise one, never mind two of them.

"Twins?" I asked breathlessly.

Michael glanced over at me and squeezed my knee, as if to tell me to calm down and that everything would be all right. But he had been through raising a kid before. This was my first, and now, I had to push two big heads out of my vagina?!

The doctor cleared her throat. "Actually, two boys and a girl."

I sat up, feeling like my eyes were about to pop out of my head. "You're kidding me."

I stared at her in disbelief and shook my head. This couldn't be true. She had to be lying. There couldn't be three babies inside of me.

"Triplets," the doctor said, pointing to the screen and showing us all three.

She started talking, but I couldn't seem to listen to a thing she was saying. My mind was buzzing and reeling with so many questions, so many thoughts, so many worries.

*Triplets? We are having fucking triplets? How are we supposed to raise three babies if we are both busy, either working or at school for eight hours a day? One of us will have to stay home—I will have to be the one to stay home. How am I going to finish school? Will I get to finish school?*

"Mia?" Michael asked. "Are you okay? You're white."

"We're having three babies? There's no more, is there?" I asked the doctor.

She gave me a huge smile and shook her head.

"Breathe, Mia," Michael said to me, stroking my knee.

"Michael, how are we going to raise three kids?" I asked, my heart beating faster and faster, my chest tightening in fear. Deep down, I knew that we could, but it was going to be a lot of work. And by a lot, I meant, *A LOT*.

Since Melissa was pregnant, too, she was going to need someone to take care of her baby when she went to work. Being a single mother was tough; I'd watched Mom do it for so long … but watching four babies? Who was going to be able to do that alone?

The doctor excused herself and shut the door behind her.

"Three babies, Michael," I whispered, shaking my head. "That's so many. What are we going to do?"

Michael cupped my face in his soft hands. "Breathe," he told me again, this time *demanding* I did so.

I took a deep breath and blew it out, trying to clear my mind.

"We will figure it out. We always do. I already told you that I'm going to ask my boss for a work-from-home position, so I can watch the kids while you go to school."

"But, Michael, I …"

"You what, Mia? What's wrong?"

I gnawed on the inside of my lip. "I'm scared," I whispered. "What if I'm a bad mom? What if I can't take care of three babies? I'm going to have to push *three* of them out of …" I gestured to my vagina and scrunched up my nose.

"*We* will be taking care of three babies, not you," Michael said, trying to get it through my head that I wasn't alone in this, like my mom had been. He would be there for me every step of the way, and he'd take his responsibility seriously, unlike Dad or Mason.

My lips trembled, and he brushed his thumb against them.

"We'll get through this. It'll be difficult, but think about having three babies of our own. A small little family. Watching them grow up together, go off to school, play sports, graduate."

I softened my rigid gaze and leaned into his touch.

Three kids … we were really having three kids.

# CHAPTER 7

MIA

"Three?!" Melissa asked, jaw dropped to her chest. She grabbed a cart and walked with me into Babies-4-Days, a local shop that only sold baby items. "Holy fuck. Mia, that's so many. How are you going to take care of them, all while going to school?"

I blew out a deep breath. "I don't know. I'm kinda freaking out. Michael says he's going to see if he can work from home, but I don't know if his boss will let him. And … ugh …" I blew out another breath, full of steam today. "And my wedding dress isn't going to fit right—I just know it. I feel like everything is so close and coming up so quickly."

"You could move the wedding back, you know," she said, pushing the cart down an aisle. "It won't hurt. You can still go on your honeymoon now and have a wedding later."

My lips curled into a frown. We'd already booked the venue, made some food arrangements, sent out invites, even had a meeting with Hailey, the wedding planner, on Saturday. Everything was set in place. I didn't want to cancel it now. Sure, we could move it back to next year … but things would still be stressful, maybe even more so then.

We walked farther into the store, each pushing a cart, and stared at the little baby clothes.

Melissa picked one up and smiled at me. "How cute is this?" she asked. "Look at these little booties."

I smiled and found a couple outfits specifically for twins. *Do they have any triplet ones?* If anyone did, I'd probably have to order it online. I put it into the cart anyway and stared at the entire list of things Michael wanted me to look at while we were here. He'd said to get what I wanted and that we'd come back and get some other essentials later.

"Mia, you're going to look hot in your wedding dress," Melissa continued.

"If I wasn't pregnant," I said, pushing the cart toward the diapers, "then maybe I'd look hot … but my stomach will be huge in it. It fit so tightly in my last fitting. I don't know if I'll even be able to get the thing on."

"Ugh," Melissa said, playfully rolling her eyes. "Stop putting yourself down. He'll love it."

My phone buzzed in my pocket as I grabbed three boxes of diapers, knowing that it wasn't enough but that we had time to come back. I pulled the phone out, thinking it was Michael.

**Dad: Sorry for being a shitty father, Mia.**

My eyes widened at the text message, and I gnawed on the inside of my cheek. *What is wrong with him? Why apologize after years of ignoring me? Why care after not giving a damn during the hardest times of my life?*

After deciding not to answer, my phone buzzed again.

**Cam: Have you decided? Party Friday night? Chelsea is asking.**

Melissa looked over my shoulder. "Is that Cam from the guys' frat?"

I pushed my phone back into my pocket. "Yeah, he invited me to a psych grad party on Friday. I don't know if I wanna go though. Parties have not been my forte."

"I think you should go," Melissa said, looking through the variety of strollers on display. She turned back to me. "Live a little. You're not going to have time to go out that much after you deliver. It'll be a nice time to relax and chat about what you love, especially if everyone going is doing psych."

"Are you sure?" I asked.

I'd never been much of a partier. I kind of hated it, especially the frat parties that Mason would drag me to when we first started dating. I had agreed to go to a couple to please him and Melissa, though not more than a handful. But this wasn't going to be a frat party. This was a party with a bunch of people I knew and liked from work and school. It wouldn't be that bad, right?

"Girl, yes," Melissa said. She pointed out a stroller. "You like this one?" I nodded, and she continued, "I think you should go. Dad asked me to get ice cream on Friday night, so he'll be busy anyway. Go to the party. Enjoy yourself."

*Enjoy myself* ...

I didn't know if I would, but I'd go anyway. In a few short months, I knew I'd be begging to have some free time again even if it was just a few moments. I didn't want to regret passing up a fun night.

**Me: Sure, I'll be there, Cam.**

# CHAPTER 8

MIA

*I*'d said I'd be at the party, and I was quickly regretting it. It was Friday night, and I wanted to go home and sleep in Michael's arms. Okay … that wasn't the only thing I wanted to do with him. I wouldn't mind if he locked me in the bedroom for a few hours and refused to let me leave.

But he had gone out with Melissa, and I had come to this stupid party just to stand around awkwardly in the corner, like I always did. Cam had talked to me a few times already, but he talked to everyone. He was more social than I ever hoped to be, which was probably why he'd joined his frat to begin with.

Pulling out my phone to try to look busy, I saw a message from Mom.

**Mom: If your father contacts you again, let me know.**
**Me: Did you talk to him?**

I didn't have to wait long for her reply.

**Mom: Mmhmm.**

**Mom: Had a forty-five-minute chat with him. Made me want to hurl. LOL.**

My lips tugged up into a smile, and I let out a small laugh. Forty-five minutes was a long time to talk to your ex-husband after not speaking to him for years. I wondered what they'd talked about the entire time. If it was a regular conversation with Dad, it was probably more like him asking for money. But … Mom wouldn't take that, not anymore.

Honestly, I wasn't sure that I wanted to know. I didn't want him in my life anymore, and that included my headspace. Merely *thinking* about him put me into a shitty mood.

**Mom: I screamed at him for the first time, and it felt so good.**

**Mom: Ooh, GTG! James is here. He'll be so proud of me. :D <3**

I smiled wide and swayed back and forth, pushing my phone back into my pocket and trying to figure out what to talk about with the other people here. I hadn't really socialized that much ever, and I was shit at making conversation unless it was with Serena or one of the guys. Attending a party with a bunch of people I only kinda knew had definitely been a bad idea.

*What was I even thinking?*

Grabbing a water bottle from the kitchen, I leaned against the refrigerator and took a deep breath, trying to blow out all the pent-up anxiety rattling inside me. I had only been here for less than an hour, and I was ready to go home.

"Mind if I join you?" Cam asked, leaning against the doorframe.

I kicked myself off the refrigerator and forced the best smile I could muster. "Sure," I said. "I don't know anyone else here as well as I know you."

He stepped closer to me. "Don't know or don't *want* to know?" he asked, cracking a sinful smile that would've made me swoon if I hadn't had a man already.

Cam was fairly attractive himself with dark hair and even darker eyes; he'd fit right into the frat scene, probably gotten all the girls when he was in undergrad.

"You could know everyone if you talked to them," he said, taking a sip of his beer. "But you don't talk that much, do you?"

I walked over to the kitchen table, leaning against it. "Way to call me out," I joked with him, sipping on my water. "I don't know what to talk about," I said honestly.

It wasn't only that … but I'd also been getting some stares lately at my growing bump. Chelsea's friends had been avoiding me like the plague for some reason tonight.

I rested my hand on my stomach, grazing my thumb over the bump and smiling to myself. Maybe this would be a blessing in disguise. I'd have my hands full, and I wouldn't be invited to parties like this ever again.

Cam looked down at my stomach and gave me a half-smile. "Mason's?"

I nearly choked on my water when Mason's name came out of his mouth. I waved my hand in front of my face, trying to cool my flaming cheeks, and shook my head. "No, definitely *not* Mason's babies. I think I'd die if he got me pregnant."

"Babies?" Cam said, brown eyes widening. He leaned forward. "More than one?"

"Three," I said, actually kind of excited to talk about it.

Since the doctor's appointment, I'd calmed down a lot. I was still so worried about having three kids at once, but Michael was so reassuring.

"Three?!" Cam asked, biting down on his bottom lip in excitement. "God, Mia." He chuckled. "You're going to have your hands full. Do you know the gender or anything about them yet?"

"Two boys and a girl," I said. "At least … I hope." Because I'd bought clothes for both boys and a girl. "The doctor almost totally missed two of the kids in the beginning."

Cam leaned forward and started speaking about something, but I couldn't focus on him because the devil himself walked into the living room behind him. I stepped to the side to get a better view of Mason talking to Chelsea. He glanced around, as if looking for someone, and then his eyes landed on me.

# CHAPTER 9

MIA

*C*am followed my stare and stared at Mason with wide eyes as he approached. Standing up taller, Cam placed down his barely drank beer. "What are you doing here? Nobody even fucking invited you," Cam said, standing in front of me, blocking Mason's view of me and my growing tummy.

My heart pounded in my chest, an uneasy feeling sitting in the pit of my stomach. *What* is *he doing here?* It was supposed to be people from the psych grad program, and that was it. Nobody else.

Chelsea—one of the first years, like me—stepped forward. "I invited him."

Cam clenched his jaw. "Do you know who he is? What he has done?"

Chelsea rolled her big brown eyes. "Don't lie about something like that," Chelsea said to Cam, arms crossed over her chest, pushing out her boobs. "It's disgusting that you'd ever even suggest that about him. He wasn't charged. It was all fake. You can't spread lies about him like that."

Just listening to her say that Mason was innocent, that what had happened to me wasn't real, that she didn't believe all the rumors—which were one hundred percent true—about Mason hurt way more than it should've. I wanted to speak up against her, tell her it was true, but Mason was glaring at me from across the room, and ... and ... I didn't want him to try anything, especially now that I was pregnant.

"Cam," I said, tugging on his arm. "Just leave it."

"No, Mia," he said. "Everyone deserves to know not to trust him."

Mason stepped forward, and I rested my hand against my bump and stepped back, not in fear but in caution. Mason was a fucking psychopath who'd do everything he could to protect his money and his reputation.

He slammed his hands into Cam's chest, pushing him back. Cam stumbled back a few feet, almost into me, and I grabbed his bicep to keep him from fighting Mason. I didn't need that right now.

"Cam, stop, please," I whispered.

Cam looked over at me, brows furrowed together, and then he shook his head and stepped farther away from Mason, hands raised to show that he didn't want to fight. I knew that Cam could knock Mason's head off though; he was a lot bigger than Mason, which was why I wanted him in front of me and not fighting him and leaving me vulnerable for one of his stupid fucking girls to pick on and torment me.

"So what, Mia?" Mason asked, scowling. "Spreading lies about me now? Jumping from Michael to this asshole?" He looked around at everyone. "You're going to believe a slut like her?"

"We're not dating," I said to him. "Not like that's any of your business."

Chelsea stepped forward, curling her fingers around Mason's

bicep, as if she was claiming him. "You two should leave. Mason is my guest. If you don't like it, there's the door."

I stared at him, then at her. Then, I pulled Cam to the door to get the fuck out of here. Glad I had come to see how utterly blind and careless some of the people in the psych department were. But part of me was feeling a bit wary. *Why is Mason here in the first place?* He'd never hung out with any of the psych undergrads or grads before. *Was he hooking up with one to try to get me jealous, to see me again?* The thought didn't sit easy with me.

"I'm going to follow you home," Cam said. "I don't trust that asshole."

And because I didn't trust Mason either, I nodded. In times like this, I would usually wait for Michael, but I wanted to get out of here before something happened. All I could think about was protecting me and my pregnant belly from the monster of my nightmares.

* * *

As soon as I drove up the driveway, Michael opened the front door, jaw tight. I prayed to whoever it was watching down on us that Michael wasn't going to start something. I didn't think he would, but last time I'd mentioned Cam, he'd seemed a bit jealous. Bringing Cam home was definitely not what I'd wanted to do, but it also wasn't the worst idea. Mason was crazy.

I got out of the car, looking down the driveway to make sure Mason hadn't followed us.

"I didn't see any cars," Cam said, stepping out of his car. His gaze traveled to Michael, who was walking down the steps for me, hands stuffed in his pockets.

"Do you need help, Mia?" Michael asked, eyes on Cam.

I pulled my purse from the passenger side and cursed under my breath as they stared at each other. I didn't know what the fuck was happening. I wanted to go inside and forget about tonight. *Fuck Mason for* still *ruining everything.*

To break the awkward tension, Cam stuck out his hand. "Cam. Cam Hodges."

Michael shook his hand a little too firmly. "Michael Bryne, Mia's fiancé."

I placed my hand on Michael's bicep and pulled him back. "Cam came back with me because Mason was at the party and I didn't feel comfortable leaving alone," I said.

"Mason was at the party?" Michael repeated. "I thought you said it was psych grads only."

"It was supposed to be," Cam said. "Everyone else there was in the program." Michael turned to Cam, and Cam held up his hands. "Hey, I hate Mason almost as much as you probably do. He's been a dick to me since freshman year."

Michael looked at him, then back at me. "We can talk about this inside."

I nodded and watched him walk back to the front door.

Cam awkwardly stuffed his hands into his pockets. "I didn't know you had a fiancé," he said.

I waved my left hand with my engagement ring at him and smiled. "It kind of happened suddenly with us, getting married and having babies, but he's amazing."

While Cam grinned, I didn't miss the way his lips twitched down for the slightest moment.

He crossed his arms over his chest and leaned forward. "I'm happy for you. You deserve to be happy after that shithead."

# CHAPTER 10

MIA

*M*ichael hadn't said much about Cam last night. I reassured him that he was a friend, but I could still see that he was a bit annoyed, maybe upset. Whatever it was, he'd seemed to get over it quite quickly, bringing me up to the bedroom, locking me inside, and coming over and over inside me, as if he was claiming my body.

I sucked on my bottom lip, daydreaming about Michael fucking me again as we tried a bunch of different flavors of cake with the wedding planner, Hailey.

Michael grabbed a forkful and stuffed it into my mouth. "How do you like that?"

My nose scrunched up. "It's not sweet enough."

After choosing between fifteen different types of cake, we decided on red velvet. Hailey brought us into another room and started asking us about everything, down to the type of napkins we wanted.

But with this talk about the wedding and these decisions and questions and thoughts … it made me so stressed out. It was nice to get this all out of the way, but I couldn't seem to focus today. My mind wandered to my dress again and how shitty I was about to look in it in a few weeks' time.

Running my hands through my hair, I blew out a big sigh and tried hard to hold back the tears. God, all this pregnancy had made me so far was horny or a sobbing mess; there was rarely an in-between.

Michael and I had decided to keep the wedding when it was scheduled, but I didn't know if my dress was even going to fit with three humans inside of me. My stomach was growing bigger by the day, and thinking about the wedding and trying to squeeze into a small dress when I was huge made me want to ugly cry.

It wasn't that I felt disgusting. I just …

"Do you think we should move the wedding back until after the kids?" I asked him right in front of Hailey.

She glanced at us with wide eyes and excused herself from the conversation, knowing things were headed south, and then she walked over to a table.

Michael stared over at me and grabbed my hand. "The other night, you were all for having the wedding sooner rather than later. What's changed?" he asked, but there was something to his voice that I couldn't quite place.

He was probably thinking that it was Cam or Mason getting in my head. But nope. It was just me, like it always was. Over-thinking. Thinking the worst. Like usual.

I gnawed on the inside of my lip. "I don't think I'm going to look good in my wedding dress," I admitted. "What if it doesn't fit? We're still a few weeks away, and my stomach is going to be huge by then. What if I can't even get it on?"

"You have a final fitting, don't you? They can make alterations if needed."

"If needed?" I asked, trying to hold back my tears. "They're *definitely* going to be needed with this." I pointed down to my stomach.

Michael ran a hand over my stomach and stepped closer to me, dipping his head and sweeping his lips against my ear. "Either way, I'm going to rip that wedding dress off you and take you on our wedding night." He grabbed my hand and walked with me back to the table. "Now, Mia," he whispered before we sat, "we're going to sit down, and you're going to let me play with your pussy as we pick out the rest of our decorations because I know that's what you've been thinking about all morning, right?"

Heat pooled between my thighs, my heart racing fast. "Okay," I whispered.

When the wedding planner returned, we sat down at the table as she started to dive back into decorations, guest dinner arrangements, and all that *fun* stuff. Michael trailed his hand up the inside of my bare thigh, pushing up the bottom of my dress and gently rubbing my wet panties.

"So," she said, "music. Have we decided? Live music or DJ?"

"Mia?" Michael asked.

I clenched, feeling Michael's fingertips rubbing against my swollen clit. "I, uh ..."

He pushed his fingers against my pussy, picking up his pace.

"Um ..." I shot Michael—who was smirking at me—a glare. A rush of heat exploded through my body. "I haven't ... thought much ..." I grabbed Michael's wrist, feeling my nipples swell under my dress. God, what was wrong with me? "I haven't thought much about it yet."

She glanced between us, pushed her glasses further up her nose, and looked back down. "Okay, I'll need to have a final answer by tonight, so we can book it as soon as possible."

Michael pushed my legs apart, hooking one of his ankles around mine, and slipped his fingers into my underwear. He pressed them against my entrance, then pushed his fingers inside of me, plunging them in and out of me.

My pussy was so wet that I could almost hear them inside of me. I gulped and tried to act normal and calm and innocent as Hailey went on to something else that I still couldn't pay much attention to.

The pressure in my pussy rose, and I bit my lip to hold back a whimper. His pace quickened, the heel of his palm hitting my clit over and over; I could feel the tension building up.

I scooted forward in my seat, hoping that she wouldn't notice as she pushed a book toward me with a bunch of bouquets in it. "I-I like …" I looked down at the flowers.

*Calm, Mia. Stay calm.*

But in this quiet room, I could hear his fingers thrusting into my wetness every single time. He moved his fingers faster, and I shut my eyes tightly.

"The …"

He made a come-hither motion, hitting my G-spot, and my core pulsed.

"Sorry, um … this one." I pointed to some white and orange roses that would match our fall theme.

Michael continued to pleasure me, his fingers stroking my sensitive spot. A wave of ecstasy shot through me, and I tightened. I wanted him inside of me so bad. Ramming his huge cock into my pussy. Clasping around him, like I had done so many times last night. Letting him come inside of me and feeling his thick cum drip out of me.

When Hailey turned to him, he responded as if he were in total control of himself and wasn't aching for me to touch him too. He moved his fingers faster, yet he continued his conversation. Heat rushed between my thighs again. I dug my fingers into my thighs and stared down at my legs, holding my breath and praying to God that I wasn't going to—

His palm hit my clit again and tipped me right over the edge. I bit my lip so hard that it started bleeding, and I tensed up, my legs shaking under the table. Ecstasy rolled through me, my entire body tingling.

"Mia, are you okay?" Hailey asked, brows furrowed together.

Michael pulled his fingers out of me and threw a worried expression in my direction, but I could see that smirk on his lips.

I smoothed out my dress and reluctantly made eye contact with her. "I'm fine. Continue."

# CHAPTER 11

MIA

*J* stepped into the bridal boutique for my final fitting before the wedding, feeling huge as fuck. My stomach felt like it was swollen, and my tits were so much bigger than they had been during the last fitting. I was growing at a freaking astronomical pace, and I wanted to hit pause for a week, so I could walk down the aisle in peace.

As soon as we walked in, Donata, the consultant, took one look at my stomach with wide eyes that didn't make me feel any better about this whole *pregnancy during wedding* thing.

"Goodness, Mia," she said in a thick Italian accent. She was older than the consultant I'd had the day I picked out the dress, her thinning brown hair pulled into a tight bun. She took my hand and led me toward the back as Melissa and Serena followed. "You're growing so quickly. Is it twins?"

"Triplets," I said, stepping onto the pedestal.

Serena and Melissa followed us in, Melissa cradling her smaller bump, and sat on one of the couches. Was I jealous that

Melissa could pull off a baby bump and still look hot? Yes. Was I jealous that her stomach wasn't nearly as big as mine was even though she was farther along? Extremely yes.

The consultant grabbed my dress from the rack and held it in front of me. "You're going to have your hands full," she said to me, then nodded to the other room. "Let's get you fitted again. See what kinds of alterations we could make to the dress to help it fit you, so you feel sexy."

I blew a strangled breath out my nose. Sexy? She'd have to work wonders for me to feel sexy in this thing. I didn't even think I'd be able to get it past my hips. It was supposed to be so tight.

We walked into the fitting room, and I tugged off all my clothes, staring at my naked body in the mirror. My stomach was beyond swollen, my skin stretching farther than it ever had before. If I hadn't been about to get married and hadn't had all this damn stress from wanting to impress everyone, I would've been happy with how I looked. It was a crazy yet beautiful thing to be able to grow babies inside of me.

Donata held the dress open and let me step into it. I pursed my lips as she slid the dress up my legs and torso. My tits were nearly spilling out of the dress, as she tried to pull it tight in the back to zipper it but failed.

"It doesn't fit, does it?" I whispered. "It doesn't zip."

My mind was racing with a thousand thoughts about how the wedding was only a week away, how we couldn't push it back now, how fucking terrible I looked in this thing.

She pushed some hair out of my face, grasping on to my arms. "Mia, you look beautiful. Stop it. Just because it doesn't fit like it did doesn't mean it looks bad on you." She gave me her best smile. "You're growing babies inside of you. It's a wonderful thing. I bet Michael is going to love this dress on you either way. I can make alterations to this dress, so it fits you perfectly for the big day."

I gnawed on the inside of my lip and frowned. "Can we go show my friends?"

"Of course, dear," she said, picking up the train of my dress.

We walked out into the room, and Melissa smiled, tears filling her eyes.

"Oh my gosh," she whispered, holding a hand to her mouth. "I never got to see this on you. It's so beautiful."

My lips tugged up in an unsure smile, and I looked at myself in the mirror. "Do you really like it?" I asked, smoothing out the fabric over my hips. It might not fit the way I wanted it to, but … but it didn't look as bad as I'd thought it'd look.

Serena grinned. "Your tits look so big," she said, wiggling her brows. "Michael won't be able to—"

Melissa gave her a side-eye. "I don't wanna hear about what Mia and my dad are going to do together," she said.

Serena cut me another grin, and I could feel my cheeks heat up. Michael had already told me exactly what he was going to do with me once the wedding was over, and horny, pregnant Mia hadn't been able to keep it off her mind lately.

Shaking my head, I turned back to the mirror. "I don't know if I'll be able to wear this the entire night. It's going to be tight," I said. Who knew if I would grow even more by then?

The boutique door opened, and James walked into the room. "I'm not late, am I?" he asked, giving me a big smile. "Mia, you look amazing, sweetheart!"

"What are you doing here?" I asked, turning around.

He hobbled in with his cane—a huge improvement from his previous walker—and looked at Donata. "You haven't told her?" He turned back to me as Donata disappeared into the back. "Your mother told me that you didn't know if you'd like the way your dress fit or if you'd be able to wear it the entire night since it's restricting, so …"

Donata came back out with a flowy off-white wedding dress and handed it to him.

"So, I thought I'd find you a dress that you could eat in and have a fun, easy night in after you walk down the aisle," he said. Tears welled up in my eyes as James handed me the dress. "Why don't you try it on?"

I shook my head. "I can't accept this. I ..." I covered my mouth with my hand and bit my lips, so I wouldn't let out any cries. This was one of the sweetest things anyone had ever done for me. "It's so expensive, and I ..." I shook my head, unable to believe that this was real.

After Dad had left, I'd never thought Mom would find someone who loved her *and* loved me too. And James doing this, buying a dress for me because Mom had told him that she didn't think I'd want to spend the entire night in such a restricting dress ... it was more than Dad had ever done for me.

"Nonsense, Mia," James said. "Go try it on."

Donata ushered me to the back and pulled off the dress I'd get married in, telling me that she'd get right on the alterations. I pulled on the boho-style wedding dress, feeling so free in it, and let out a small giggle, unable to hold back my excitement.

When we walked back out, James nodded and gave me a wink. "There you go," he said. "I hope you like it. I went through hundreds of them to find one that I thought you'd like."

"I love it," I whispered.

# CHAPTER 12

MIA

*A*fter I thanked James and nearly cried my eyes out for how happy and grateful I was that Mom had someone like him in her life, Serena drove us back to her place for a last-minute bachelorette party.

Michael had said he didn't want a bachelor party, that he'd already experienced that once in his life and he didn't need to do it again. As far as I knew, he was going out with a couple guys from work tonight, like he did occasionally for a beer.

We sat on the couch, watching movies and drinking lemonade. I might've dropped a couple slices of an orange into the drink, satisfying all my cravings. I lay back on the couch and smiled to myself. Everything seemed as if it was getting back to normal. This was how it had been before Melissa found out I fucked her dad and I found out she'd been sleeping with my boyfriend at the time.

Now, things were so much simpler.

Serena sat up and paused the movie. "Okay, we can't do this all night. Let's gossip."

I nearly snorted and pushed myself back up to a seated position with some help from the couch. Yep, life was definitely getting back to normal. "What do you want to gossip about?"

"Cam," Serena said with a smile on her face.

"Cam?" Melissa and I said in unison.

"Cam," Serena said, wiggling her brows. "How is he? Has he found a different girl to obsess over yet, or is he still hitting on you, knowing that you're getting married to a hottie?"

I shook my head. It had been a few weeks since that party, and I hadn't gone back to another one. At first, I'd thought it would be a bit awkward to go back to school and my internship with him, but he made sure to not make it awkward at all. In fact, we had grown closer in a friendship kind of way.

"He was never hitting on me. We're just friends."

Serena playfully rolled her brown eyes. "I think he likes you," she said, twirling her hair around her finger. "He definitely checks you out, stares at you like he likes you. It's the same way Victor stares at Melissa."

Melissa rolled her eyes. "Victor does not stare at me like that."

Serena smirked at me. "Both Victor and Cam definitely do."

"No, he doesn't," Melissa and I said again.

I pulled an orange slice out of my lemonade and bit into it. "When I told him about Michael a few weeks ago, he looked happy for me but sad too," I admitted.

It'd kind of made me feel bad because Cam was actually one of the nicer guys I'd met in college, but there was nothing anyone could do that would make me fall out of love with Michael.

"I guess he might like me?" I brushed it off like it was nothing. "But it doesn't matter. I'm taken." I turned to Melissa. "You're not."

"Victor does not like me," she said again, shaking her head and getting all defensive. "And I don't like Victor either. I appreciate his help with everything, but we will never get back together."

The way she couldn't keep eye contact with either of us told me that she was lying straight through her teeth.

"Well …" Serena said, hopping up from her seat and walking to their apartment door. "I guess you're going to really *hate* this then. I wanted to invite the guys to this bachelorette party, but I had one condition …"

She yanked open the door, and Damien and Victor walked into the room, each looking bored out of his mind with nothing but a pair of suit pants on and a bow tie fastened around his neck.

"Goddamn, Serena, we've been waiting for you out in the hall for fifteen minutes."

A laugh escaped through my lips, and I could just imagine all the people walking up and down the hallway, staring at them.

Serena playfully slapped Damien's chest. "Come on. Do what we practiced! It's Mia's bachelorette party!"

Serena started some slow, sensual music, and though they seemed to not want to be here, the guys started dancing in a really bad *Magic Mike* kind of way. I sucked my bottom lip into my mouth, trying to stop the tears of laughter from running down my cheeks.

*God, I love them.*

# CHAPTER 13

MIA

"You wanna see my dress?" I asked, plopping my pregnant ass right on the edge of Cam's desk.

It was my last day of the internship and school before the wedding and before Thanksgiving break. Cam had been asking me almost everything about the wedding, the babies, and the dress, so I thought that it was finally time to show him, as I wouldn't see him for the next few weeks.

He closed his laptop and leaned back in his seat, tapping his pen on his knee. "You know I've been waiting to see it," he said, staring at me with big, dark eyes.

I pulled out my phone and pulled up the side-by-side picture of both the dresses that I'd be wearing during my wedding. I handed him the phone, butterflies in my stomach. We were so close to the wedding. I couldn't wait for it. And then we were planning to honeymoon in Greece for two weeks.

He grabbed my phone from me, eyes widening at the picture. "God, Mia," he said with a smile on his face. His cheeks turned the lightest shade of red when he looked back up at me. "You look so beautiful in them."

I smiled as I remembered what Serena had *joked* about the other night at our party with the guys. Cam couldn't really *like*, like me, could he?

"Thanks," I said, taking the phone back from him.

"Michael will love it."

"You think so?"

He scratched the back of his head, messing up his brown hair. "I would, if I were marrying you."

We stayed silent for a few moments, a heavy tension in the air between us. I deposited the phone into my pocket and gulped, resting my hand on my bump almost instinctively.

Cam sat back up and cleared his throat, biceps flexing. "Sorry, I didn't mean to make it weird." He looked down at his phone, then up at me, licking his lips. "I just ..." He paused for a long time and looked away again. "Never mind."

"What is it?" I asked.

"Nothing," he said, shaking his head. "I'm happy for you. Really." He glanced back up at me and gave me a genuine smile that I had never really seen before; it almost looked vulnerable, coming from such a huge frat boy. "Fine ..." he said eventually, blowing out a breath through his nose.

I sat up straighter and leaned forward.

"I've always been jealous of Mason," he started.

My nose scrunched. That was not what I had expected to come out of his mouth.

"I ..." He clasped his hands together. "I always thought he treated you badly. I told him that if he didn't start treating you better, you'd leave him. I knew you deserved better—everyone did—but he didn't want to listen to what I had to say. When I found out that you and he broke up, I thought that it was my chance to finally ask you out. I wanted you to find someone to treat you right, someone like me."

My heart stopped for a moment. I parted my lips to say something, but nothing would come out. I pressed them back together and shifted, my heart warming. What could I say to something like that? He must've liked me for a long time, and now, he'd found out that I was both engaged and pregnant with triplets.

"I don't know what to say," I whispered.

He shook his head and gave me his best smile, but it didn't reach his eyes. "You don't have to say anything to me, Mia. I'm happy for you. Any man in my position would be."

Something about his voice sounded so sad, and I wanted to reach out and comfort him. But I didn't because that would be beyond disrespectful to Michael. Instead, I gave him a smile that didn't reach my eyes either.

"I'm happy that you found someone who can take care of you," Cam said. "I hope your wedding is everything you've ever dreamed about and more."

# CHAPTER 14

MIA

*M*ichael's lips swept against the back of my neck, his hand lightly placed around the front of my throat.

"Don't stop," I breathed, my voice quiet and raspy. The morning sunlight flooded in through the window, and I pushed my hips back against his. "Please, don't stop."

It was Friday, the day before the wedding, and Michael had taken off work to spend time with me. He ran his hand over my stomach and slipped it under the bump to tease my clit with his fingers. We hadn't been able to keep our hands off each other all week, yet Cam had kept wandering through my mind every now and then.

I was sad for him, but I didn't feel bad that I was already taken. I'd never feel bad about Michael.

He pumped into me faster, fingers rubbing rougher circles around my clit.

"Michael," I whispered, curving my back.

Michael took a steady breath through his nose and set his lips against my ear, thrusting himself into me. I moaned.

"Say my name again, Mia," he mumbled against my neck, his stubble making me shiver in delight.

I dug my fingers into the bedsheets, and he left a lingering kiss on my skin.

"Michael," I whispered.

He gently placed his fingers on my chin and moved my head, so he could press his lips to mine as he pumped in and out of me faster.

"You drive me fucking crazy," he whispered on my lips. "I can't wait to fuck you senseless every morning and every night we're in Greece. On the balcony. On the beach. Every inch of the hotel room."

My pussy tightened around him as my hips moved with his, and I grabbed his hand that was fondling my pussy and intertwined our fingers. He trailed our fingers up my side and drew me even closer to him.

Harder and faster, he pumped into me, making me clench down on him and tense in his embrace. The pressure rose higher and higher, and I cried out against his lips. He slowed down, his thrusts long and deep.

"Oh God, just like that," I said.

He continued to ram into me, hitting my G-spot with his huge cock almost perfectly.

"Come inside of me, please."

He groaned in my ear and rested his forehead against my cheek, coming inside of me. Feeling his body shudder against mine, I let out a loud moan and found myself unraveling. I tilted my head back and felt pleasure rolling through me.

"In twenty-four hours, you'll be my wife," Michael murmured against my lips.

"Twenty-four hours?!" I asked, scrambling to get out of bed. "I have to go."

He curled his arm around me and pulled me closer. "Come on, Mia. You don't actually believe that we have to not see each other for twenty-four hours beforehand, do you?" He buried his face into the crook of my neck, his stubble grazing against my skin.

I shivered and relaxed into him, glancing at the clock and seeing that we had a little longer than a day left. "You just don't want me to leave," I said, playfully poking his stomach.

He chuckled against me. "You're right," he said, finger snaking around the front of my throat. "I'd rather you stay in this bed all day with me, so I can take you any way and anytime that I want."

A laugh escaped my lips, and I pushed him away. I had to go to James's home. Mom was waiting for me there tonight. James had signed her out of the assisted living home earlier this morning, and she had been texting me nonstop about coming over to celebrate with her.

After escaping Michael's hold, I jumped off the bed and pulled on some clothes. I pressed a kiss on his lips and grabbed my to-go bag. "I have to go, really, Michael."

"Next time I see you, you're going to become my wife." He pulled me into another long, hot kiss. "I've been waiting for this for months, Mia. I can't wait."

# CHAPTER 15

MIA

"Good morning, sweetheart!" someone said from my bedside.

I mumbled Michael's name into my pillow and scooched backward to touch him. All I wanted to feel were his big, strong arms wrapped around my body, him pulling me against him, his breath on my ear, his mouth on my skin, his cock against my—

The lights flickered on and off, and then someone jumped on the bed next to me.

"Wake up!" Serena said. "Your mom and James made breakfast for the bride!"

I blinked my eyes open and saw Mom sitting in her wheelchair at the foot of the bed and Serena basically on top of me in her pajamas.

"It's my wedding day," I whispered, sitting up a bit too quickly but caught myself before I could fall back. "I'm getting married today."

Serena helped me out of the bed, and we headed toward the kitchen with Mom. James's kitchen table was packed with French toast, pancakes, fruit, and eggs—everything that I used to love as a kid and everything that would make me bloated as hell today.

Sitting down in a chair, I furrowed my brows at Serena. "Where's Melissa?" I asked.

"With Michael," she said. "She said she'd be over a bit later."

Mom and Serena chatted during breakfast as I struggled to eat any food because my stomach was in knots, just thinking about today. I was about to make the commitment of a lifetime to one of my best friends, to the father of my babies, to the man of my damn dreams. It felt surreal. I felt like I was living in some kind of fanfic romance I used to read online when I was younger.

The doorbell rang, and my stomach tightened even more.

"Ooh, makeup and hair are here!" Serena said, hopping up to get the door.

Two women walked in with a bunch of boxes and makeup kits, calling out, "Good morning," to all of us.

James excused himself, and I helped Mom clean off the kitchen table.

"You know, I'm so excited for you," she said to me as Serena sat in the chair to get styled first. "I wish I could walk you down the aisle today, and I was going to ask James to do it for you ... but you don't need anyone to *give you away*. You make your own decisions, and you've made good ones to lead you here."

Tears welled up in my eyes, and I begged myself not to cry. My eyes would look all red and puffy today if I did.

Mom grabbed my hands and smiled at me. "You've found yourself an amazing man, and I can't wait for you to love him for the rest of your life. After everything that you've been through, you deserve to be happy and smiling every moment of every day. And Michael has been the only one to make you that way."

"Mom, stop," I whispered, pressing my lips together as the

tears threatened to spill down my cheeks. I wrapped my arms around her and pulled her into a tight hug.

If it wasn't for her, I wouldn't be here today. She had helped me become stronger. She had helped me become me. And I would never be able to thank her enough for doing that.

# CHAPTER 16

MIA

We stood in the center of a white stone bridge at Carolds Farm on the day of our wedding. The bridge overlooked a lake and miles upon miles of flower-decorated land, right outside the city. Michael was a few feet away with his back turned to me for our first look.

"Okay," our wedding photographer said.

She glanced at me with a huge smile, and I rubbed my sweaty hands together and stared at the back of his head. I'd decided last minute to have a first look before the wedding, feeling as if it would be more intimate to see Michael for the first time in my wedding dress before everyone else saw me.

"You can turn around, Michael."

My heart raced as Michael turned around to look at me. Everything seemed to slow down, and I saw so many emotions in his widening eyes. He attempted to suppress his grin behind a small smile, but it didn't work. He took a deep breath, taking me in and shaking his head.

"God, Mia," he whispered, stepping closer to me, one hand resting on my hip. "So much for spending twenty-four hours apart," Michael murmured into my ear, his hands sliding around my waist. He pushed some hair behind my shoulder and gave me the same breathtaking smile he had when he found out I was pregnant. "You look amazing in this dress. Too bad I'm going to have to rip it off you later."

I smiled and rested my hands on his chest, fingers toying with his bow tie to straighten it for our pictures. "Not this one. I have another one for the reception." I gnawed on my bottom lip. "Easier access."

"Don't tease me like that right before you walk down the aisle," Michael said, making me feel all sorts of things. "You know that I'd take you right here, turn this into a boudoir shoot instead of wedding pictures."

I playfully rolled my eyes and smacked him on the chest. "Not so loud," I whispered.

He wrapped his arms around me and pulled me even closer. "Louder?"

My cheeks flushed, and I grinned cheekily up at him. "No!"

After taking about fifty wedding pictures with our photographer, Hailey appeared at the base of the bridge with a huge smile on her face. "I have to steal Michael away from you," she said to me. "It's almost time!"

Michael pressed a kiss on my lips. "See you soon, Mrs. Bryne."

I watched them walk away and toward our indoor ceremony. I ambled back to my entourage inside the building.

Serena squealed when she saw me, clapping her hands together. "Oh my God, I'm so excited!"

Hailey reappeared at the door. "Is everyone ready?" she asked, gaze landing on me. "Mia, how are you feeling?"

My stomach was in damn knots, but the good kind.

After giving me a curt nod, she ushered everyone to their spots, and the classic wedding music started. I clutched my flowers tightly and stepped forward, waiting for Hailey to push me out there to get married already.

White roses lined the aisle, orange flowers hung from the ceiling, and Michael stood at the altar. My heart pounded inside my chest, and I walked toward the crowd of people.

*Holy shit, this is really happening. I am marrying Michael Bryne. I am having kids with Michael Bryne. I am finally making my life mine.*

When I made it to the beginning of the aisle, I locked my focus on Michael and smiled widely. I didn't particularly like all the attention from a bunch of people I barely knew. Hell, I didn't like the attention at all … but when I saw him, everyone else seemed to disappear. It was cliché, but I had never felt anything like it.

I held my flowers tighter and walked down the aisle toward my future. After everything that had happened in the past year, I was truly happy that this was how my life had turned out.

Mom grasped James's hand and grinned at me as Serena and Melissa watched from the altar. I approached Michael, my heart pounding in my chest, and stood directly in front of him, my eyes on nobody else and nothing other than his deep gray eyes, his slightly graying dark hair, those little lines on his face.

I didn't care about what anyone else thought about us. I knew that we were meant to be. Maybe we'd had a rough start. But maybe sleeping with your best friend's dad wasn't *all* that bad. It had its highs, and it had its lows. And so I made the commitment of my life and said those two little words that would change everything.

"I do."

# CHAPTER 17

MIA

*T*wo hours into the wedding reception, I had changed into my new dress, had my first dance with Michael, and eaten dinner with all my friends. We talked about the babies and the wedding, the honeymoon we were leaving for in two days.

Michael leaned toward me. "Meet me in the hallway," he whispered. "Five minutes."

After excusing himself from the table, he grabbed his drink and walked over to some of his friends from work, keeping his icy stare on me.

Five minutes … five minutes, and there wasn't any doubt in my mind that he'd take me to the back room and fuck me senseless, like he'd promised.

"I so wish I got to go to Greece," Melissa said, slumping back in her seat.

She tilted her head to the side, and I watched her gaze meet

Victor's, who stood across the room with Damien and a couple of Michael's relatives.

Michael placed his drink down on a side table, and I stood up, my heart racing in my chest. Why was I doing this with my mom and friends here? Because despite it being my wedding day, I was still that same old *horny for Melissa's father* Mia.

Fuck five minutes. I wanted to get railed now.

"I'll be back," I said, hurrying to the hallway where Michael was waiting for me. "Michael," I whispered, looking around.

Suddenly, he pulled me down the hall toward the back room. People were scattered and chatting in the main ballroom. The doors closed behind us, and I sucked in a breath.

"We can't do it here. There are people we know in the other room! Our entire families!"

Michael wrapped his hand around my waist and tugged me to him. "I told you what I'd do to you once we were married," Michael said, kicking open the back room door with his foot and pushing me into the room. "I'm not going back on my word now."

As soon as the door closed behind us, Michael had me flush up against it, his raspy breath in my ear. "Fuck, Mia," he said, hands all over my body. "Thank God that you changed." He pulled up the back of my flowy reception dress and undid his suit pants enough to pull out his hard cock.

He let spit drip from his lips onto his dick and rubbed it against my aching pussy. I placed my hands on the door and arched my back, pushing my hips toward his and hoping it'd slip right inside of me.

I clenched when he pushed an inch into me. He reached around my body and groped my breasts through the dress.

"I should've fucked you out in the hall," he murmured against my ear, making me tighten. "I should've taken you as soon as I fucking saw you earlier."

"God, Michael, give it to me."

He pushed another inch of himself inside of me. "I'm going to make love to you on our balcony in Greece." He placed a hand on my lower back, his finger curling around my ass. "Your bare tits bouncing against the railing, legs trembling, pussy quivering around my cock as I fuck you for everyone to see."

I dug my fingertips into the door until they turned white. "Please," I whispered.

Another inch.

"Tell me what you want."

"Put your dick inside of me," I said. "Now."

He pushed himself all the way inside of me until his hips met mine, and a wave of pleasure rolled through my body.

Someone jiggled the doorknob, and I almost tensed. Placing a hand next to mine on the door, Michael didn't stop. He continued to trail his hot mouth down the column of my neck. He slid his other hand over my mouth to muffle the moans that I couldn't hold back.

"Shh, shh, shh," he whispered into my ear. "Don't want anyone to hear my wife moan my name."

*Wife.*

The word made me tighten around him. *I am Michael Bryne's wife, Mrs. Bryne now.* My heart fluttered at the mere thought of being his and him being mine.

Our bond was already beyond strong, but this solidified all the feelings we had for each other. Michael was going to be by my side forever and ever, through thick and thin, when I was at my lowest and at my highest. He'd be with me through it all, and I would be by his side every step of the way.

Someone jiggled on the door again, and Michael pressed his palm against the wooden door even harder, his muscles tightening through his dress shirt. He continued to pump in and out of me, his husky voice whispering sweet nothings in my ear.

Whoever was at the damn door didn't go away. Instead, the

door shook, as if someone had bumped into it. I could hear raspy breaths and quiet moans coming from the other side.

"Fuck it. Get in the restroom," Victor said on the other side.

My eyes widened. I knew that there was nobody, except one person, who Victor would be hooking up with at this wedding. But thankfully, Michael hadn't heard it. Or if he had, he didn't say anything, because he continued to pump into me, his hand wrapped around my waist, gripping me firmly.

"I'm going to come inside of you, *Mrs. Bryne.*"

My pussy tightened even more around his cock, and I threw my head back. The pressure rose in my core with every thrust. I was seconds away from unraveling for the first time around my *husband.*

"Please," I whispered.

He groaned against my ear and slowed down. I dug my fingers into the door until they turned white and moaned louder. My pussy pulsed over and over on his cock as I came undone around him.

When he was finished, he pulled my underwear back up my thighs and let my dress fall back down to cover my ass. He turned me around and leaned against the door, standing beside me. One hand on my stomach, one brushing the hair out of my face, he stared at me with the biggest smile on his face. "I've been waiting so long for this day."

"Our wedding?" I asked with a smile.

"Getting to call you my wife," he said, grabbing my hand and opening the door. "Come on, before anybody gets suspicious."

We walked back out to head down the hallway. When we passed the women's restroom, Victor and Melissa walked out together, Melissa's hair ruffled so badly that it looked as if she wasn't even trying to hide the fact that she and Victor had just hooked up.

Her face turned bright red when she saw us. "Dad," she whispered. "We were, uh ..." She stumbled over her words, as Michael narrowed his eyes at them, raising one dark brow. "We were just—"

I hooked my arm around hers and pulled her toward the ballroom. "Freshening up," I said to save her from the embarrassment of admitting it out loud.

I pulled her ahead, and Michael and Victor fell behind.

"What happened to *I don't like Victor?*" I teased, throwing her words right back at her.

She playfully rolled her eyes at me, cheeks still flaming. "Oh, stop it. You know I have this entire time." She looked at her feet when we walked back into the ballroom, where everyone was chatting. "But you know, I fucked up big time. We might've gotten together, but I have to make up for a lot of shit. Nothing will be normal between us for a long time."

I gave her a soft smile back. "I guess that's life ... but, hey, you'll get there one day. You'll get the wedding of your dreams with the man of your dreams. I promise it'll happen." Because ... I'd never thought it'd happen to me, but it had.

Life had a certain way of making things better when you were sure it had gone to absolute shit.

# CHAPTER 18

MIA

"I never thought I'd spend Thanksgiving Day at a bar in Greece," Michael said from across the table.

Sitting on a rooftop bar that had a breathtaking view of the Acropolis, I sipped on my water with orange and stared at Michael's sculpted face as the candle flickered off it and made it glow. "I never thought I'd spend *any* day in Greece."

We had been on our honeymoon for about five days now, and it was everything I'd ever wanted. We'd traveled around to see a bunch of towns, ancient structures, where the original Olympics had been held, Delphi, and so many other beautiful places.

I was glad I hadn't pushed the wedding back. It was great to get out before the babies came. I knew that once they did, I wouldn't have any time at all.

"I've been thinking a lot about us and how we're going to raise three kids," Michael said, sitting across from me. "I want to spend more time at home with them, and I know you need to be able to get to school and labs without them on your hip."

I reached over to brush my thumb over his knuckles. "And?"

"And I asked my boss for a work-from-home position starting in January until I can get my own structural design company started up."

"Michael, that's wonderful!" I sat up. "I didn't know you wanted to start your own company."

He gave me a breathtaking smile from across the table. "Who doesn't want to spend as much time as they can with their family and build a life for them?"

* * *

"LAST NIGHT," Michael said to me, his hand sprawled over my stomach as I ate baklava on our balcony in Karpathos, over-looking the ocean. After a week of staying in Athens and a couple other ancient cities I'd always wanted to see, we were on a quiet island, just … relaxing.

It felt good to get away from all the drama for once, and this vacation was everything that I could have ever asked for. I had Michael, three babies on the way, and an upcoming career in psychology.

Michael's phone buzzed on the table beside us. Michael ignored it, telling me that he just wanted to relax, but then my phone started buzzing a few moments later. I glanced down at it, seeing Melissa's name pop up on the screen. She hadn't messaged us at all these past two weeks. I knew she wanted to give us space.

This must've been important.

After handing the phone to Michael, he put it on speaker.

"Is my dad there, Mia?" Melissa said over the phone, her voice shaky. She let out a long grunt and whimpered, sounding like she was in pain.

Michael sat up, leaned over on his forearms, muscles flexing. "I'm here."

"I think that I'm having contractions. I tried to ignore it, but I … they're coming faster and faster."

Michael tensed. "Are you headed to the hospital? You're a couple weeks early," he said to her.

"Victor is bringing me right now," she said.

Michael looked at me, brows furrowed together, as if he was unsure about what to say or what to do.

I leaned forward. "We'll be home as soon as we can, Melissa."

She sounded heartbroken. "I'm sorry. I promised you that I wouldn't bother you … but I didn't know what to do."

Although she'd promised not to bother us all vacation, knowing that we wanted some peace before the kids came, she wasn't bothering us. This was serious, and we only had a day left here anyway.

"It's okay," I said to her. I didn't mind it at all. "We only have a day left. We can come back a day earlier for you and your baby."

After I hung up, I cradled my bump and hurried to our room to pack our suitcases as quickly as possible. Thankfully, since we were supposed to leave tomorrow, I had packed the majority of our things up. I didn't know if we'd find an earlier flight, but I sure hoped we did. I knew Michael didn't want to miss the birth of his first grandchild.

*Grandchild* sounded so weird. Was I considered a grandma now? I wasn't even a mother *yet*. Melissa's son would be growing up with his aunt and uncles. It was a bit weird to think about, but at least they would have someone to play with, right?

Michael walked into the room, pushing his phone into his pocket in a hurry. "I booked the flight. It leaves from Athens in two hours. We're going to be pressed on time," he said. He grabbed the suitcase from me. "You're pregnant, and this is heavy, Mia."

"I can do it," I said. "I don't need your help."

"Go make sure that we have everything from the other rooms," he said, nodding to the door. "I'll do this."

I gave him a side-eye and searched through the rooms to make sure we didn't forget anything. I grabbed the bottles of wine and alcohol that I wanted to try from Greece once I gave birth and made sure Michael packed them.

When we were sure we had everything, we hurried to our taxi and rushed to the airport, hoping we would make it on time. The last flight from Karpathos to Athens was going to leave in half an hour, and then our flight from Athens would leave about an hour later.

I didn't know if we'd make it before Melissa gave birth, but we'd try.

# CHAPTER 19

MIA

Serena threw her arms around my shoulders as soon as Michael and I got to the hospital room. She and Damien were gathered in the waiting room, standing patiently for any news from the doctors.

"Did she have her baby yet?" I asked, brows furrowed together.

Serena shook her head. "Victor is in there with her. She's in labor now."

Michael curled one arm around my waist. "How long?"

Serena looked at Damien, then back at the hallway, grimacing. "About fifteen hours now. They should be getting close, right?" Serena asked, looking up at Damien, who shrugged because he sure as hell didn't know.

"Melissa took thirteen hours," Michael said, glancing down the hallway toward the delivery rooms.

I rested a hand on my stomach and felt one of my babies kick.

I would be here sometime soon, giving birth to not one, but three, which kinda, sorta terrified me.

Part of me wished that I were with Melissa in the delivery room to give her support, but Victor was good for her. Maybe they were beginning to patch up their relationship, and while he might not be the father, I knew that he loved Melissa with all his heart and that he'd do anything for that baby.

He was more of a man than Mason ever was.

"Did you have a good honeymoon?" Serena asked, taking a seat.

I smiled at her and grasped Michael's hand. "It was beautiful, except for the two snoring teenagers we sat next to on our flight back." I yawned, not having gotten any sleep for almost twenty-four hours. From the time change to those annoying brats, I felt like I was about to drop at any moment.

A nurse walked down the hallway, a clipboard in one hand and a smile on her lips. "Melissa Bryne's family?" she said.

We all stood.

"Melissa gave birth to a beautiful boy. They're both healthy and doing well. You're welcome to come see her."

I pushed Michael along, knowing that he'd want to be the first one in there with them, and looped my arm around Serena's, leaning my head on her shoulder. Everything seemed like it was falling into place.

When we walked into the room, Melissa was holding her baby in her arms, her cheeks stained with tears and runny black mascara. Victor stood next to her, one hand on Melissa's shoulder and a small smile on his face.

"You came," Melissa said to Michael. "Mom didn't even answer the phone."

"Of course I came," Michael said to Melissa, smiling at her and the baby. "What's his name?"

"Archer," she said, sitting up and handing him to Michael. "Here."

Michael gently took Archer in his arms, cradling his head and rocking him. I grinned as I watched how gentle Michael was with a baby. My stomach fluttered with butterflies, and I couldn't wait until I gave birth and Michael was staring down at *our* children like that.

# CHAPTER 20

MIA

To say that Melissa was an over-the-top mother would be an understatement. She had moved back in with us, wanting to give Serena and Damien their space, and had been throwing mini parties every week for the baby. It was cute, and I was really glad that she had changed into a greater person, but … it was a little too much for me, especially when I was about to pop any day now.

My patience was running thin. My back was hurting like hell. My breasts were aching. I wanted to give birth already, so I could get back to a normal-ish life.

I held Archer in my arms and stared down into two big baby eyes. Archer looked almost exactly like Melissa, except those eyes. They reminded me of the devil. But I guessed I'd have to get used to them. Mason couldn't rule my life forever.

"One month," Melissa said, gently poking Archer on the cheek and watching him smile. Michael stared at us from across the kitchen table, lip curled up. "You're one month old today, my baby."

"Do you thi—" I started, but then I heard the slightest pop and felt wetness pool between my legs. My eyes widened, and I handed Melissa her baby. "Oh my gosh," I whispered, standing up and thrusting a hand between my legs.

Wet.

I was wet.

Michael stood to his feet almost immediately and hurried over to me. "Your water broke," he said, scooping up my hand in his, grabbed the hospital bag he had packed a couple weeks ago, and hurried with me to the car. "Melissa, meet us at the hospital when you're finished here. Call Mia's mother."

I grasped my tummy, both so afraid and so excited for this whole pregnancy to be over. I knew that once the babies came, we would barely have any time together, but I wanted to meet the little humans I had been growing inside me for the past nine months.

We made it to the hospital in three minutes flat. Michael had driven so much faster than he usually did that I was damn surprised we hadn't gotten pulled over and I hadn't given birth in the front of his car.

They got me into a room almost immediately, and the contractions that had started intensifying in the car were suddenly almost unbearable, coming every few minutes, each one lasting longer than the last.

"Michael," I said, gripping his hand, "I'm so scared."

He leaned on the side of the bed, lightly cupping my chin. "It's going to be fine, Mia."

"My vagina is about to be torn in two," I said, holding my stomach as another contraction hit me so much harder than the last. I took deep breaths, trying to remember how they'd taught me to breathe in that pregnancy class Melissa and I took together.

"Okay, Mia," the doctor said, pulling on a pair of gloves, "it looks like these babies are ready to come now. Take a couple deep breaths because you're going to start pushing."

I did my best to mentally prepare myself for this, wishing Mom were with me, but she and James were probably on their way. He had to pick her up from the assisted living place, but I couldn't wait much longer so I started to push.

"You're doing great, sweetheart." Michael seized my hand in his and pushed some hair off my sweaty forehead.

I squeezed my eyes closed and pushed as much as I could.

"Keep pushing for me. You're so close."

Piercing pain shot through my body; my pelvis felt like it was splitting in half. I held his hand tighter and pushed as hard as I could until I heard a baby crying. I relaxed onto the bed, a tear falling down my cheek as the doctor cleaned off the boy.

"Don't get too comfortable, Mia," she said to me. "You have to push out two more."

She handed me the baby for a moment, and I held him to my chest. "Aiden," I whispered as the tears started to flow down my cheeks. I couldn't hold them back, couldn't stop them from coming out.

My stomach tightened again, and I handed him to Michael, knowing that I was about to give birth to baby number two. I breathed heavily, clutching the rails of the bed.

"Holy fuck," I said through gritted teeth. This was the worst damn pain that I had ever experienced.

Michael must've handed the baby to a nurse because he was right by my side again, gripping my hand and whispering all those lovely things into my ear. It didn't make this any easier, but it made me want to push with even more force and continue.

"A bit longer, Mia," he said to me. "You're so close."

I pushed harder, and after a few moments, I found Mav in my arms, a full head of hair already on his tiny head, like Aiden. He cried louder than Aiden had, but they already looked so similar. I knew it was going to be difficult telling them apart.

"Last one," the doctor said to me. "You're gonna push one more time for me."

Tears streamed down my face, and I was positive I wouldn't be able to push anymore. My chest was heaving up and down, and I felt like I could barely breathe. I wanted nothing more than for this birthing thing to be over with already.

"Push, Mia," Michael said. "You can do this."

I let out an agonizing scream and pushed for as long as I could, thinking about how my life could've turned out if it wasn't for Michael. I'd have been in a relationship without love, without happiness, without any kids.

"You got this," he said to me. "One last time."

I heard a baby crying, and a little girl was set in my arms.

"Sadie," I whispered, staring up at Michael with tears in my eyes.

I hugged Sadie to my chest and let all the tears fall.

I was happy. So fucking happy.


**THE END**

# ALSO BY EMILIA ROSE

**PARANORMAL ROMANCE**

Submitting to the Alpha

Come Here, Kitten

Alpha Maddox

My Werewolf Professor

The Twins

**CONTEMPORARY ROMANCE**

Poison

Stepbrother

**EROTICA**

Climax

# ABOUT THE AUTHOR

Emilia Rose is an international best-selling author of steamy romance. Highly inspired by her study abroad trip to Greece in 2019, Emilia loves to include Greek and Roman mythology in her writing.

She graduated from the University of Pittsburgh with a degree in psychology and a minor in creative writing in 2020 and now writes novels as her day job.

With over 18 million combined book views online and a growing presence on reading apps, she hopes to inspire other young novelists with her tales of growth and imagination, so they go on to write the stories that need to be told.

Join Emilia's newsletter for exclusive news > https://www.emiliarosewriting.com/

# ACKNOWLEDGMENTS

Thank you to Jamie Beedle for suggesting the amazing series title <3

Made in the USA
Middletown, DE
15 March 2023

26696353R00158